THE MASK OF ZORRO

THE MASK OF ZORRO

A NOVELIZATION BY JAMES LUCENO
STORY BY TED ELLIOTT & TERRY ROSSIO
AND RANDALL JAHNSON
SCREENPLAY BY JOHN ESKOW AND
TED ELLIOTT & TERRY ROSSIO

POCKET BOOKS
New York   London   Toronto   Sydney   Tokyo   Singapore

An *Original* Publication of POCKET BOOKS

POCKET BOOKS, a division of Simon & Schuster Inc.
1230 Avenue of the Americas, New York, NY 10020

ISBN: 0-671-51989-1

First Pocket Books printing July 1998

10 9 8 7 6 5 4 3 2 1

Printed in the U.S.A.

In memory of my *compadre* and
frequent collaborator,
Brian Daley

Acknowledgments

Thanks, once again, to Dan Slater, of Pocket Books, for his editorial skills; and to Sandra Curtis, John Gertz, and Ben Kaplan of Zorro Productions for their kind support; and a tip of the rapier to Lucia Robson and Dan Hart, who provided much-needed background on Old California.

THE MASK OF ZORRO

In Old California

STORM CLOUDS HAD BEEN BUILDING THROUGHOUT the afternoon, casting gloom on an already dark day. But neither the hulking thunderheads nor the threat of deluge were enough to keep the people of El Nuestra Señora de Reina de Los Angeles from gathering in the plaza to vent their rage over the pending execution of three of their own. After suffering years of abuse at the hands of the Spanish commandant of Los Angeles's meager presidio, the people had grown accustomed to cruel injustices, but by inviting death into the pueblo on the very eve of his departure, Comandante Rafael Montero was adding insult to injury.

Clenched fists rose defiantly into the dust that swirled above the square, and a chorus of furious denunciations reverberated from the plaza's surround of stately buildings. Wielding nothing more lethal than sticks and tools, the pueblo's boldest and bravest faced off with a squad of soldiers whose sharpened bayonets glinted in the waning light.

1

"Liberty, equality, independence!" the crowd chanted, taking up the rallying cry of independent Mexico. Emancipated from Spain and eager to assert dominion over its vast holdings to the north, Mexico stretched from the Texas frontier with the United States west to the Pacific Ocean, including the territories of Baja and Alta California.

Alejandro and Joaquin Murieta, though only eight and ten years old, respectively, weren't strangers to the inequities of Montero's brutal reign. Crouched in the darkness of a canvas-covered wagon that sat in one corner of the plaza, they had the rough-and-tumble look of wolf cubs long separated from the pack. They were barefooted and dirty behind the ears, but their eyes held a sparkle that was at once ingratiating and mischievous.

"Hurry, Alejandro, cut it," Joaquin urged his younger brother. "Cut it before we're too late to see anything!"

The stronger of the two despite his age, Alejandro punched his crude knife through the wagon's cover, and as the stout blade cut a ragged hole in the canvas, the angry chanting of the townspeople swelled, as if the voice of one instead of many.

"Liberty, equality, independence!"

Alejandro pressed his left eye to the hole he had fashioned and squinted at the plaza, where the soldiers were advancing on the crowd, flourishing their bayoneted flintlocks. Walling the plaza on the north, reared the *cuartel general,* where the soldiers were garrisoned; and diagonal to that stood Comandante Montero's own residence, with its glazed windows and balconies adorned with intricate wrought-iron railings.

"Hurry, *hermano*," Joaquin repeated. "Cut another hole!"

Alta California's sudden change of overseers mattered little to the brothers, who had been raised at the nearby San Gabriel mission among Yang Na Indian neophytes. Of mixed blood, they had never thought of themselves as belonging to one nation or another. While it was rumored that they were now residents of Mexico rather than New Spain, they remained orphans just the same, without a silver *real* to their names and with only as much education as Fray Felipe and the other padres had seen fit to dispense.

The second eyehole completed, Alejandro flattened his face to the rough cloth once more, feeling momentarily as if he were actually wearing the wagon's entire black cover like a mask.

"My turn!" Joaquin announced, shoving him away from the holes so that he could have a look outside. After surveying the scene for himself, he moved to allow Alejandro access to one of the holes while he squatted by the other.

As they watched, an older boy named Pepe tore from the crowd and began to shinny up the plaza's flagpole, where a tattered Spanish flag snapped in the wind. A stout corporal broke ranks to restrain him, only to be forced back by the pressing throng, undaunted by the corporal's bladed flintlock. In moments, Pepe had ripped the flag from its perch and the wind had carried it to the paving stones below.

"Use it to clean your floors!" someone shouted at the soldiers. A cheer went up as a second person dashed for the flagpole and the green, white, and red flag of Mexico was unfurled and raised.

Alejandro wondered if the cheering was of any

3

consolation to the three condemned men, who stood blindfolded and bound to posts on a raised wooden platform situated along the front wall of the *cuartel*. For just then, to the martial cadence of a single drum, a six-man firing squad was marching briskly through the garrison gate to take up positions opposite the men, their tall hats and braided uniforms in stark contrast to the sombreros, serapes, and frayed cotton of the townspeople. The bare arms of weeping women reached imploringly past the bayonets toward the grim-faced soldiers.

"Have mercy," a young wife pleaded. "Have mercy."

Alejandro glanced worriedly at his brother. "He had better come soon. Or else—"

"Caramba, what's taken hold of you two!" a harsh voice interrupted. "Cutting holes in my wagon cover!"

Silhouetted against oblique light pouring through the wagon's suddenly opened rear flap, Señor Lopez, the pueblo's undertaker, stood like the Reaper himself, shaking a scythelike finger at the damage Alejandro's knife had done. "This a place of dark business," he went on, gesturing behind him to the coffins that waited to be occupied, "not a place for sport!"

"We're sorry, señor," Joaquin was quick to say, as he and Alejandro scurried toward the rear of the wagon. "We were only hoping to get a look at Zorro."

Lopez's shoulders hunched even higher than normal at mention of the bold renegade who had fought Rafael Montero at every turn. He glanced furtively to both sides before looking at the brothers again. "Mind your tongue, *chico*—especially here, under the very gaze of the commandant."

4

"But he'll come, won't he?" Alejandro pressed in hushed urgency. "The Fox will rescue them, no?"

The angular features of Lopez's gaunt face set. "Someone clearly thinks that he will try." Again he gestured to the coffins, which smelled strongly of freshly planed pine. "Have you not yet learned to count?"

Alejandro eyed the boxes, counting silently to himself. *"Four!* You mean—"

Lopez tugged a shroud from one of the coffins, exposing a large *Z* that had been engraved into the soft wood and painted black. The boys spent a moment gaping at the mark that had made Zorro a legend from Santa Barbara to San Diego. Alejandro's blood turned cold at the thought of Zorro lying dead inside the box.

He was stepping through the wagon's open flap when Lopez said, "I built boxes for your mother and your father. I would hate to have to build boxes for you as well." The undertaker paused for a moment, then added, "Hurry back to the mission. There's nothing for you to see here."

Rafael Montero decided that the time had come to put in an appearance. Not down below in the plaza, of course—what with the rabble emboldened enough by the sight of the Mexican flag to be pelting his soldiers with rotten fruit and small stones—but from the salon balcony of his *casa mayor,* where he might at least present a more difficult target.

Activity swirled about him on all sides, as servants and Indian slaves rolled up tapestries and rugs and packed the last of the household items in huge chests and shipping crates. The brigantine that was to carry

5

Montero around the Horn and on to Spain would set sail the following morning, and several wagonsful of his personal belongings had yet to be delivered to the beach at San Pedro.

"Take special care of the cellar stock," he cautioned one of the Indians. "For every bottle of wine I lose, the skin of your back will suffer tenfold." Still managing to look uncomfortable in civilized clothing after some five years of service, the Indian returned an awkward bow, an unreadable expression on his dark, high-cheekboned face.

Montero gave a downward tug to his fine waistcoat and walked to the balcony. A trim but broad-shouldered man nearing forty, he carried himself with the grace that came with entitlement and the arrogance that came with command. He had nothing but contempt for the indigenous peoples of the New World, who in his opinion would seldom work unless threatened and whose blood had tainted that of the race who had vanquished them from Mexico to Peru. And so, in an effort to coax more "industry" from them, he had been compelled to treat the mestizo population with equal bluntness, levying taxes and punishment as needed.

On the balcony, he stepped into full view of the crowd. Stirred by a southeaster—the bane of the big ships that put in at San Pedro harbor, several leagues to the west—the air was warm and humid, redolent with the scent of wildflowers and orange blossoms. After more than fifteen years as a Californio, Montero had come to appreciate the fragrances, and he knew that he would miss them, as he would the vineyards and the cool evening breezes. Fast between snow-covered mountains and the turbulent ocean, Los Angeles was as close to paradise as Montero had ever

6

come, but in spite of it all, there were things he was glad to be putting behind him.

"Death to Montero!" some in the crowd shouted upon seeing him. "Death to Montero!" Pieces of rotten fruit spattered against the shutters to either side of him, but he refused to give anyone the satisfaction of seeing him flinch.

Spain had begrudgingly slipped the yoke from Mexico's neck a year earlier, in August of 1821, but the news had only recently been received in California. Now the fledgling republic was in the hands of "El Libertador," Agustín de Iturbide, along with those of an aristocratic upstart by the name of Antonio López de Santa Anna. It was unlikely that Spain would so much as recognize Mexico's independence, and Iturbide's treasury was already depleted, but even Alta California, nearly as remote from Mexico City as it was from Madrid, had become an uncomfortable place for those who remained loyal to the Crown. Even more so for Montero, whose tenure as comandante had been plagued almost from the start by a black costumed outlaw, whose horse ran as swiftly as the wind and whose sword had left its mark in the stucco of many a wall, and in the flesh of many a soldier.

As if reading his thoughts, the townspeople surged with palpable fury against the meager line of presidio troops who were holding them at bay, and several more pieces of fruit flew past Montero's head and shoulders.

"Your aim is as hopeless as your future," he muttered. "When Iturbide leaves you to rot on the vine like California's grapes, you'll pray that I was still in command—taxes or no."

* * *

The undertaker's comment resonated in Alejandro's thoughts as he and Joaquin wormed through the crowd in search of a clear view of the trio of bound men. *I built boxes for your mother and father* . . .

High above the plaza, Comandante Montero stood still as a target in the center of his balcony, while overripe oranges, lemons, and tomatoes painted the white walls at his back.

Nearing the edge of the crowd, where the jostling was at its most fervent, the boys found their circuitous path blocked by none other than Father Felipe himself, who was on his way to administer a final blessing to the condemned. A thick-set man with more hair on his brow than on his head, he advanced on them like an angered bull.

"Get back to the mission, you little cowchips," he scolded. "This is no place for children."

"But—" Alejandro started to say when Joaquin nudged him in the ribs.

Father Felipe planted his work-hardened hands on his hips. "But what?

Alejandro gulped and found his voice. "But we were only now on our way to the mission, Padre." He gestured broadly. "As you say, the plaza is no place for children on a day like this."

The priest's eyes narrowed in distrust. "On your way, were you? Then perhaps I'll just see you along."

He reached out, as if to take them both by the scruff of the neck, but the boys were too quick for him, and in a blink they had squirmed back into the forest of legs, losing themselves in the crowd. Emerging on the far side of the plaza some moments later, they found Hector, Ramon, and some of the pueblo's other lowborn sons enacting their own version of the excitement, using puppets painstakingly crafted from wood and papier-mâché and costumed with bits of cloth.

Comandante Montero was center stage just now, face-to-face with his nemesis, Zorro, who was outfitted in mask, flat-crowned hat, and cloak—though cotton died with blackberries substituted for the satin the real Zorro was known to wear.

"Do you think I am frightened by your puny sword and your silly mask?" Hector was saying in the deepest voice he could muster from his thin chest. "I am Comandante Montero. Everyone must obey my laws and commands, for I command many soldiers."

Ramon, the voice of the Zorro puppet, countered, *"I* will not obey you, Comandante Montero. Because, because you are . . . stupid. And dumb—"

"Wait, wait," Alejandro said, brazening his way through an audience of children older and larger than him. "Stupid and dumb are words *we* throw at each other. Besides, they mean the same thing. Zorro would say—" he puffed out his chest "—I spit in your face, Montero. *Death* to the Spanish high boots. Wherever I carve my mark, the people know that—'"

The rest of Alejandro's words were buried under the thunderous sound of approaching hoofbeats. He whirled in time to see three horsemen spurring their steeds into the plaza, heedless of the townspeople or the soldiers, to say nothing of Hector's puppets, which were crushed under the horses' hooves as the children flung themselves to all sides to avoid a like fate.

Alejandro recognized one of the riders as Don Luiz Ortíz, *patrón* of the most wealthy cattle ranch in all of Los Angeles. With him rode his foreman and another *vaquero*. The three reined up in front of Montero's *casa mayor,* just below the balcony on which the

9

seemingly bemused commandant stood. Don Luiz placed his hands on the silver pommel of his tooled saddle, dismounted in a rush, and hurried into the grand house.

"Ruined," Hector was saying of his puppets. "Even Zorro."

The Mark of Zorro

MONTERO GLANCED OVER HIS SHOULDER AS DON Luiz hastened through the parlor toward him, redfaced and out of breath.

"Your Excellency, I just learned of the executions," the cattle rancher began. "But you've no time for this. Soldiers from Santa Anna's army are even now on their way north from San Diego—"

Montero turned and held up his hands, no more ruffled by the news than by the jeering of the peons below. "Compose yourself, Don Luiz. Take deep breaths." He paused to demonstrate, gracefully lifting his hands as he inhaled. "Picture a quiet pond, surfaced with water lilies . . ."

Don Luiz blinked in confusion, then snorted. "Yes, yes, but you must leave—now!"

Montero faced the plaza once more. "Of course. Only one final duty to perform for the Crown—as well as for myself."

Don Luiz stepped out onto the balcony. "Be sensible, Rafael. Why trouble yourself with a couple of tax evaders at this late hour, when you should be safely aboard the ship that awaits you."

Montero cut his eyes to Luiz. "Tax evaders? But haven't you heard? These three are insurgents. They have been judged guilty of conspiring to commit acts against the Crown."

"But the Californias are now under Mexican rule."

"Perhaps. But Los Angeles remains under my rule until I leave. And I won't tolerate insurrection."

In the plaza, the sublieutenant commanding the firing squad was barking orders to his six troops. The wailing of the victims' wives and daughters grew louder as the Franciscan, Father Felipe, began to mutter prayers and move his right hand in the sign of the cross.

"Mexico may one day thrive without Spain," Don Luiz remarked, "but Alta California will never be the same without you."

Montero smiled faintly. "A temporary condition, my good friend. In the meantime, I have something for you." From inside his waistcoat he drew a sheet of impressed parchment, which he handed to Luiz. "In compensation for your years of devoted service."

The rancher examined the parchment in mounting bewilderment. "A land grant. But I don't understand. These hectares are the property of the Crown—"

"Yes. And by tomorrow they will be the property of the Mexican government—unless I turn them over to you." Montero paused for a moment. "I know de Iturbide. He trusts that the dons will be dutiful taxpayers, and he will respect your claims." He motioned to a table in the salon, which held a stack of similar grants. "The remainder of the territory has been divided equally among the other dons. You will make certain they receive the grants, no?"

12

Luiz moved to the table to inspect the documents, then glanced up at Montero.

"What is it, Luiz?

"It's only that . . . the land you've given me. It's little more than high desert scrub. And yet you favor the others with lush, arable—"

"One day you'll understand that I have favored *you* above all, Don Luiz." Montero smiled enigmatically. "You need only cooperate with the new commandant and whatever magistrates the town elects."

"But to be governed by *peasants . . .*"

Montero's look hardened. "Peasants with rifles and cannons, Luiz. Peasants who will keep the peace until I return." He placed his hands on Luiz's shoulders. "Was not this land named after de Montalvo's imagined treasure island? Rest assured, my friend, California is richer than anyone knows, and upon my return I will show you just how rich. We're not going to allow de Iturbide or Santa Anna to prevent us from realizing our destiny. You have my word on that."

A shrill whistle sounded, and Montero turned and stepped to the wrought-iron railing. "Remove the children from the plaza!" he shouted down to his troops. "Then proceed with the execution." Looking over his shoulder at Don Luiz, he added, "Children should not be made to witness the things we do—no matter how wretched they are."

Alejandro fought a losing battle against the friar who was hustling him from the plaza. Soldiers had taken hold of Joaquin, Hector, and Ramon, all of whom were protesting the rough treatment as vociferously as Alejandro. Others were crying, in fear of what the soldiers might do to them.

"But someone has to prevent the killings, Father,"

13

Alejandro said while he squirmed in the Franciscan's powerful grasp.

"Don't worry yourself, young one," the friar told him softly. "Someone will."

Ceasing to struggle, Alejandro cast his eyes to the ground dejectedly. As he did, he noticed that the friar wasn't wearing his usual sandals, but black leather boots and silver spurs, whose rowels gleamed from polish. Moreover, the tip of a scabbard showed where black silk trousers disappeared into the left boot. Alejandro lifted his gaze to the friar's face, which, though somewhat concealed in the darkness of his brown cowl, wore a black mask across wide-set eyes and an aquiline nose.

Alejandro's heart hammered in his chest. "But you're—"

Zorro shushed him. "That's to be our secret, no?"

Alejandro swallowed audibly. To see Zorro was one thing; but to be speaking with him . . . He grasped for words, but his tongue failed him. He could only nod his head repeatedly.

"Good," Zorro said.

The masked man gave him a reassuring pat on the shoulder, turned, and disappeared into the crowd. Alejandro's heart continued to beat wildly in his chest. He wanted to follow, but he knew that Joaquin would never forgive him. Instead he raced back to where he had last seen his brother and began to scout around, only to bump into him not fifteen meters from the plaza. In a rush of words, he explained what he had seen, and Joaquin immediately suggested that they climb to the roof of the *cabildo*—the magistrates' building—where they were certain to have the best view of the plaza.

By the time they reached the forward lip of the

14

cabildo's tiled roof, the commander of the firing squad was raising his drawn sabre.

"Preparen!" the officer ordered.

The six troops cocked the hammers of their muskets and the three prisoners straightened at their posts, determined to face death with honor and dignity intact. Alejandro and Joaquin scanned the plaza for some sign of Zorro.

"Apunten!"

The soldiers raised the muskets to their shoulders and took aim, forefingers stiff at the triggers. Panic took hold of the families of the condemned, and the crowd roiled in hatred and frustration.

The commander's arm came down like a felled tree: *"Fuego!"*

With a loud *crack!* that many in the crowd mistook for flintlock fire, the braided tail of a black leather whip coiled itself around one of the guns. The wielder of the whip gave a sideways pull that yanked the musket into the one adjacent to it, which in turn slammed into the next gun in line, and so on, until all six muskets were no longer pointed at the hapless prisoners but at the squad leader, whose eyes bulged in terror a moment before the fusillade found him.

"Zorro!" Alejandro shouted from the roof as the sharp smell of discharged gunpowder permeated the afternoon air.

"El Zorro!" someone in the crowd yelled. *"Viva El Zorro!"*

With his whip recoiled, Zorro leaped onto the platform, his rapier drawn and eager to dole out justice. Cries of recognition and relief surged from the crowd as California's cloaked avenger rushed to the prisoners, freeing them from their bonds with swift slashes of his weapon, before turning to confront those sol-

15

diers who weren't fumbling black powder into their flintlocks for another shot.

Steel met steel as Zorro's blade deflected bayonet lunges on all sides. Nimble as the fox that was his namesake, he countered each thrust with parries and counter-ripostes that instantly sent two of the soldiers flailing back with hands clasped to bleeding puncture wounds and angry slashes. When a third was fool enough to draw his saber, Zorro turned the attack to him, enveloping the soldier's blade and winging it from his grip.

On the roof, the sudden ringing of an iron bell roused the Murieta brothers from dumbstruck exhilaration. Turning to the source of the sound, they saw Montero, still on the balcony, with his hand on the striker of a large, wall-mounted bell. In obvious response to the signal, a group of soldiers edged out onto the balcony of a turret below the boys to take up firing positions on the plaza.

"A trap!" Joaquin said.

Alejandro returned a wide-eyed nod. "The fourth casket! They mean to kill Zorro!"

Joaquin gazed about him, then gestured to the near corner of the roof, which supported a stone statue of an angel. "Maybe we can push it over!"

Quickly, they scampered across the terra cotta tiles and put their backs into the labor of loosening the statue from the mortar that held it in place. After a moment, the mortar gave and the statue plummeted from the roof, felling the soldiers before they could fire.

His attention drawn by the crash, Zorro winced as he sustained a substantial gash in the arm; then, disengaging, he vanished into a building, while soldiers shouldered through the crowd in mad pursuit.

16

Belly down on the forward edge of the roof, Alejandro and Joaquin were waiting for Zorro to reappear when hands sheathed in black leather dropped down on their shoulders. Twisting in their grip, the boys found themselves staring up at the Fox himself.

"My thanks to you, *compañeros,*" he said, showing a grin beneath the mask. Then he removed a medallion that hung from his neck and handed it to Joaquin.

Wordlessly, Joaquin held the medallion up for his brother's inspection. The piece was engraved with an intricate, puzzling design of concentric circles, crisscrossed by intersecting lines.

"Pura plata!" Alejandro said in awe.

Zorro nodded curtly. "Silver and much more." Again he laid a hand on their shoulders, but now with the lingering touch of benediction. "Now, if you'll excuse me, I am late for my own party."

And with that, he turned and calmly stepped off the roof.

"You should have known that Zorro would interfere," Don Luiz was saying as Montero counseled him to retreat to the safety of the parlor. "He'll be a thorn in your side until the end."

As he has been for twelve years, Montero thought. Ever since Montero had undermined the power of the town's magistrates and proclaimed himself sole authority over military and civil matters, much as the governor of Monterey had in the wake of its sacking by French privateers only three years earlier.

Montero gestured dismissively. "You underestimate me, Luiz. I was *counting* on his showing up. What better way to coax the Fox from his lair than by threatening to kill three members of his brood. Now,

17

my friend, remain inside while my soldiers rid me once and for all of this 'thorn.' "

Returning to the balcony, Montero caught a wisp of movement from the corner of his eye and turned in time to see a black shadow flit from a nearby rooftop, leap nimbly to a ledge, and alight on the very balcony on which he was standing, drawing a rapier in flight. Montero extended his neck somewhat as the tip of Zorro's blade pressed against his throat, but he neither flinched nor recoiled.

"No matter what the peons think," Montero strained to say, "you are a man, and not an apparition."

Zorro leaned toward him, drawing a drop of blood from Montero's neck. "You would murder three innocent men just to capture me?"

Montero glanced at Zorro's wounded arm. "I would gladly murder one hundred to see you in irons."

Zorro smiled tightly. "Fortunately for California, you no longer enjoy that prerogative."

Montero returned the insolent grin. "Spoken like a true *gentleman*—outlaw."

Zorro's blade switched through a lightning-quick zigzag movement, and Montero grimaced in pain. "Three men, three cuts," he said. "A small keepsake of Los Angeles, *Rafael*. To remind you never to return."

The masked man stepped back, sheathing his sword, then sounded a whistle that echoed across the plaza. An imposing black stallion appeared through the crowd, making its way toward the balcony. With a touch of gloved fingers to the broad brim of his hat, Zorro sprang from the ledge onto the horse's saddled back.

"Away, Tornado," Montero heard him shout above cheers from the crowd and the reports of a few muskets that failed to find their black-clad mark.

Zorro rode the horse up a flight of exterior stairs. Silhouetted against the setting sun, Tornado reared, pawing the air with his forelegs while Zorro waved his sword gallantly in a gesture of victory.

Overwhelming the soldiers, the townspeople spilled across the plaza to cheer on their champion.

With teeth clenched, Montero staggered to the balcony railing in time to see horse and rider leap to the flat roof of an adjacent building and disappear from view. Taking his hand from his slashed neck, he found on his palm, emblazoned in blood, the mirror-image of a Z.

Montero cursed and shook his fist at the heavens, vowing revenge on his nemesis, the masked man who had been the scourge of his existence.

Zorro Unmasked

SPURRED BY THE EVENING'S EVENTS, TORNADO COV-
ered the few leagues between Los Angeles and the
coast at full gallop. Zorro surmised that he wouldn't
be pursued—not with Santa Anna's soldiers on the
approach—but he took all the usual precautions
nonetheless: tarrying in a copse of willow short of the
bridge that spanned the Río de Los Angeles de la
Porciúncula; doubling back on his own trail; scanning
the dark countryside from the crest of the grassy ridge
that separated the inland basin from the cold waters
of the Pacific Ocean . . . He performed each maneu-
ver with his customary prudence, and yet there was
something other than vigilance at work that night;
something closer to the heart-tugging sentiment of
loss than one of concern for his safety. For it had
occurred to him that his years as "the Dark Angel of
Alta California," "the Defender of Justice," had finally come to an end. Rafael Montero would be
leaving on the tide, and with him would go the host of
injustices he had perpetrated in the name of the

Spanish Crown. The Californias belonged to Mexico now, a nation with little tolerance for absentee kings or petty dictators. The Fox would pass into history, or better yet into legend, where he truly belonged, and Diego de la Vega would have his life back at last.

"God be thanked that Montero returns to Spain," he said, patting Tornado's thickly muscled neck. "You and I are getting a bit long in the tooth for acts of derring-do."

Having run off most of his excitement, Tornado picked his way down the final rise above the beach, snorting happily and shaking out his mane in a steady wind that promised rain before midnight. The salt air was heavy, and the surf turbulent. For the past half-hour, horse and rider had been crossing de la Vega land—some 12,000 hectares, awarded to Don Alejandro de la Vega twenty years earlier by the King of Spain. Like so many other aristocrats who had arrived from Europe, Don Alejandro had become a *ganadero*—a cattleman—eventually amassing a sizable herd of the short-legged, sharp-horned cattle that were descended from the piebalds, blacks, and tan and reds the conquistadors had brought to the Americas.

Shortly, the de la Vega hacienda came into view, enticingly lit by lanterns and oil lamps. But Tornado moved instead toward a thirty-meter-high waterfall that plunged over jagged stone, some distance from the elegant house.

The curtain of thundering water concealed the entrance to a giant cavern Diego had discovered quite by accident as a youth, and which had remained his and Tornado's secret since. Its existence, however, had been known to the original owners of the hacienda, who had not only shored up the interior of the cave but had joined it to the main house by means of a secret passageway and a short flight of stone stairs. The story went that the wife of the owner had been deathly afraid of attacks by Indians, and had employed the cave as shelter during those times when her unwarranted apprehension got the best of her. Thus young Diego had found the cave to be well stocked with water, bushels of dried corn, books, and two aged muskets.

Early on the cave had been little more than a setting for imaginative boyhood games, but it had gradually become a place he sought out in times of confusion or reflection.

The mouth of the subterranean chamber—a tall, narrow crevice—afforded just enough headroom for Diego to remain atop Tornado, but he dismounted a short way along and removed the horse's saddle and tack. Torchlight illuminated a large alcove strewn with hay that served as Tornado's stall, and from which he was free to wander outside for water or grazing whenever the mood struck him. Beyond the alcove, the cave opened into a large vaulted room that was part library, part workshop. But it was the floor, comprised of an ornate, raised dais, that most attested to Diego's handiwork. An area of some one-hundred square meters of marble tile, its inlaid design of concentric circles replicated the engraved medallion he had bestowed on the two urchins from the San Gabriel mission. The silver piece was itself a gift bestowed on Diego by Sir Edmund Kendall, the brilliant fencing master under whom he had studied in Madrid.

Ridding himself of hat, mask, and cloak, Diego cleaned his rapier and placed it in a rack that held similar short swords, along with several epees and a broad sabre. He then changed out of his silken costume and continued to the rear of the shadowy grotto where he had built a small shrine to the Virgin.

With his height, his lean frame, and handsome features, Diego cut a dashing figure, even stripped of his cloak and hat. Kneeling in front of the shrine, he lit a pair of tallow candles that flanked an ivory statue of the Virgin, crossed himself, and uttered a short prayer that gave thanks even while he asked forgiveness for his acts of violence, their justification notwithstanding. The prayer was a ritual he never failed to perform, though one he had long been eager to surrender.

Diego's thoughts drifted back to a decade earlier. It was upon his return from university schooling in Madrid that he had first donned the fabled mask of Zorro, cut from a bolt of Oriental satin he had purchased on a whim in Barcelona the night before his ship had sailed for Cape Horn and the Californias. Summoned home by his father, Diego had had nothing more than the beautiful Esperanza on his mind for the whole of the months-long voyage. Was she betrothed? Had she thought of him? Would she receive him again, as she once had?. He had no sooner stepped from the longboat that carried him from ship to shore when he had begun to hear of the tyranny that had come to Los Angeles and the neighboring pueblos, in the form of Rafael Montero. Indians had been persecuted and killed; *vaqueros* and peasants had been brutalized and forced to pay exorbitant taxes; even the dons had been obliged to stand mute while Montero had dissolved the magistrate and appointed himself governor-general of the district.

The arrest of Alejandro de la Vega, who had himself served a term as governor, for striking Montero, had firmed Diego's resolve to undermine, if not topple, the commandant from his unmerited perch. It had been clear to him from the start that the other dons and caballeros, no matter the extent of their discontent, were averse to being viewed as revolutionaries. And so Diego had been left to thwart Montero on his own, and in a manner that wouldn't call down the wrath of the Crown on his father or bring shame to the rest of his noble family.

A fox that had taken up residence in the cave during Diego's sojourn in Spain had provided the name for his secret identity. Swift and wily, with keen eyes and even keener hearing, the fox eluded pursuers by racing off in zigzag courses. Moreover, he made his den in the ground and did his hunting at night. But the true inspiration for Zorro had come from oft-told tales of sharp-clawed, black-cloaked apparitions who roamed California's valleys and mountains, creating mayhem and striking terror in the hearts of unwary travelers. . . .

His prayer completed, Diego ascended the stairs that led to the hacienda and triggered the spring-and-pulley mechanism that swung open a slate door at the back of the deep hearth in the parlor on the first floor. A button concealed under the parlor mantel activated the slate from the house side, the accidental discovery of which had supplied Diego with his own new world.

The parlor was deserted. A narrow room with broadplank flooring, it was furnished with high-backed chairs, a sanctuary bench, a *trasero* cupboard, and other pieces of massive furniture the late Teresa de la Vega had brought from Castille at the turn of the century. Diego quietly crossed the room to a doorway in the opposite wall and peeked in.

Elena, just two years old, was asleep in her crib, under the watchful gaze of Morning Dove, the child's devoted nursemaid. Morning Dove looked up from her spindle whorl to show Diego a smile that was at once warm and inscrutable.

"Do you think she's warm enough?" Diego asked.

"I always put on an extra blanket." Morning Dove rose from her chair and moved for the door, her plain skirt brushing against the sprigs of romania she had lashed to the balusters of the crib.

Diego took her place by the crib, gazing lovingly on the infant. "I should explain why I wasn't here to tuck you in and kiss you good night," he began in a whisper. "You see, dear little one, there were three men who were much in need of rescue, and who else but your father could effect their release? Ah, but you should have seen me in action, cutting their bonds with my sword and battling the ones who would have shot them. And then there was the evil man behind it all. Like a cat, I made a jump to the balcony on which he stood like some unassailable monarch, and I drew my blade and placed it to his throat like so—" Diego plucked a stalk of romania from the bouquet and brandished it like a sword "—saying to him, 'You would kill three innocent men just to see me captured?' And the evil man said—"

Diego swung around to a sound in the doorway and found Esperanza gazing in on him, as he had gazed on Elena a moment earlier. A striking woman in whom classical beauty and robust nature found equal expression, Esperanza looked radiant in the soft glow of the lanterns. But even in that romantic light, Diego could see that the long wait for his return had tormented her, even after so many years of safe

25

returns, of seeing to knife, sword, and hardball wounds that always mended, of sanctioning and oftentimes abetting the fight he had taken on. . . .

"I was waiting on the veranda," she began. "I thought I'd see you ride up." She exhaled and smiled. "But continue your account, husband. 'The evil man said . . .'"

Diego cleared his throat. "He said . . . something of little consequence."

"And the good prince—what did he do?"

"Why, he leapt from the balcony onto his faithful steed, Tornado, and he raced home to his beautiful wife, Esperanza, and his little child, asleep in her crib." His eyes returned to Elena, and he lowered his voice to add, "And he promises, now, never again to embark on foolish or dangerous actions."

Laughing affectionately, Esperanza came to him, kissing him and encircling his waist with her arm. Together, they watched their little child, who stirred and smiled in her sleep.

"Look, Diego, how she loves to hear your stories," Esperanza remarked.

"It's only the sound of my voice. One day she'll have no time to hear of my exploits."

"She already has your mischief. Just today she broke the little clay horse you made for her." Esperanza turned slightly in his direction and kissed him again, tenderly, on the cheek. "Besides, I never tire of your stories. So why should she?"

Diego gave her hand a gentle squeeze and led her back into the parlor and a short way down the hallway, toward the staircase to the ground floor. As she moved to embrace him, Esperanza leaned against Diego's wounded arm and he flinched away.

"What is it?" she asked, her eyes full of concern.

"Nothing. A scratch."

She stopped. "Diego, you promised me. No more nights waiting up, praying you'll—"

He pressed his finger to her lips. "Montero is returning to Spain, *querida*. We have fought and won. What I told Elena is true. Tonight was Zorro's final ride."

She took her lush lower lip between her teeth and showed him the skepticism in her eyes, furrowing her brow. "You've said such things before—"

"This time is different," he was quick to assure her. "I am retiring my shadow. I'm going to let myself grow old and fat, while my lovely wife raises our five children—"

"Five?" she said in mock surprise.

He waved his hand. "Five, six, as many as you want—as many as we have time to make."

Her almond eyes shone brilliantly as she looked up into his face. "Tell me more, husband. What else will we do?"

"What else? Why, we'll raise the finest cattle in Alta California, and we'll employ one hundred *vaqueros* to ride herd on them. I'll capture the swiftest mustangs and race them up and down the length of the Camino Real. We'll host rodeos and wild fandangos that all Californios will be desperate to attend."

"Will you dance?"

"We will dance, my love—like never before. The *jota,* the *jarabe,* the waltz . . . We'll be the envy of every family from here to Yerba Buena. And I'll plant olives, an orchard of Valencia orange trees, and grapes for wine, and you will cultivate perfect roses of all colors."

"Diego," she sighed, smiling and pressing herself to him.

27

He tilted her face to his and kissed her passionately, his heart bursting with a new sense of hope and relief. Only when she suddenly stiffened in his embrace did he open his eyes, reacting to her sudden disquiet, as if to something she had glimpsed over his shoulder.

Whirling like a dervish, Diego came face to face with his nemesis, Rafael Montero.

A Duel to the Death

BACKED BY TWO OF HIS TROOPS, MONTERO SMILED cloyingly as he watched Esperanza and Diego from the staircase. On meeting their gaze, he felt certain that Esperanza, out of modesty, would back out of Diego's embrace. True to her defiant nature, however, she made a point of kissing him again, holding him more tightly than before. And where, earlier, rotten fruit or the tip of Zorro's rapier hadn't been enough to make Montero flinch, he did so now.

"Dona Esperanza," he said at last. "Looking as beautiful as ever."

Before locking eyes with Montero, Diego's gaze fell briefly on the bandage Montero had plastered over the Z that had been slashed into the flesh of his neck.

"What brings you here, Don Rafael?" Esperanza asked nervously.

"Fate," he replied.

Diego affected an arrogant smile. "What an honor to have the *former* governor of Los Angeles in our home. Won't you stay for supper? Oh, but what am I thinking? You have no time to eat. You're fleeing for your life."

Montero glared at him. "What a happy man you must be, Don Diego, to be the sole object of attention of such an enchanting woman."

"A happier man has never lived," Diego returned in a voice of facile condescension.

"There was a time," Montero went on, almost casually, "when yours were not the only arms that embraced such loveliness. Why, I myself can still recall the softness of the lady's skin." He paused to demonstrate counterfeit embarrassment at a possible impropriety. "Or perhaps Dona Esperanza failed to tell you of the moments we shared while you were perfecting your . . . manners in Madrid?"

Diego's attempts to restrain himself were transparent, though he did manage to keep an even tone in his voice. "On the contrary. She has spoken not only of those moments but of other misfortunes as well." His dark, flashing eyes returned to the bandage. "If you'll bear my asking, Comandante, did you injure yourself shaving? With too fine a blade, perhaps?"

Montero sniffed. "Infantile wit was undoubtedly a close second to your studies in manners, Don Diego. Or was it third—after swordsmanship?"

Diego raised his eyebrows in false incredulity and spread his hands. "Swordsmanship? As everyone in Los Angeles can surely attest, I am a man of peace. A cattle rancher, no more, no less. Now, at the risk of being impolite, I must ask that you state the reason for your unannounced visit."

Montero looked at Esperanza. "I have come to apologize."

"Apologize?" she said, uncertainly.

"For failing to protect this territory from the peasants who have overrun it. And for failing to earn your love. And, finally, for having to deprive you of a husband." Cutting his eyes to Diego, Montero motioned to his pair of guards. "Seize him."

Diego uttered a short laugh as the guards took hold of his arms. "This is absurd, Montero. With what offense am I charged—lack of courtesy in seeing you to your ship?"

Montero advanced a step and placed a hand on Diego's wounded arm, then tightened his grip. Diego made no sound, but the wound itself betrayed him. Blood oozed through the fabric of his sleeve and left its mark on Montero's palm.

"Blood never lies—*Zorro.*" Montero stepped back, his expression a mix of contempt and triumph. He wiped his hand on the sleeve of his coat. "You are a traitor to both your country and your station. I've long suspected as much, and now I have all the proof I need." At the snap of his fingers, half-a-dozen additional soldiers crowded into the foyer. One of the troops had hold of the struggling Morning Dove, a hand clasped across her mouth. Montero gestured to Diego. "Take him away."

Esperanza tried to rush to her husband's side, only to be blocked by one of the soldiers. Montero snorted. "He is unworthy of you, Esperanza."

Diego stiffened, drew himself up to his considerable height, and threw the guards off; he at once relieved the nearest one of his sabre and lunged at Montero, who answered the sudden attack by hacking wildly but ineffectually with his own sword. Below, the soldiers went into motion, but it was obvious from their scurrying that none could manage a clear shot at their target. As Diego and Montero began to circle each other, their weapons gleaming in the torchlight, a fierce, silent understanding passed between them. The customary rules of engagement no longer applied. This was to be a duel to the death.

Esperanza screamed, clasping her hands in front of her as Montero rushed Diego, engaging him with bold cross-strokes and furious thrusts. But Diego fought as well in the clothes of a wealthy landowner as he did under the cover of mask and cloak. Almost from the start he commanded the contest, refusing to acknowledge Montero's feints or attempts at *derobement*. Steeling his blade from being knocked out of line, Diego executed counterattacks and grazing actions with dazzling dexterity. Recklessly, Montero dropped one hand to the floor in a *passata-sotto* lunge, only to have his weapon flung from his grasp by a swift, flawless envelopment. The sword clattered to the floor behind him.

Towering over Montero, Diego had begun to advance for the kill, when a muffled discharge sent a .75 caliber musket ball whining past his head and into the wall behind him. In the instant Diego recoiled, Montero scampered to his feet, ordering his men to hold fire.

"This is between us!" he shouted as he collected his sword and renewed the attack.

It was impossible to know whether de la Vega had been spooked by the musket round or if the quick disarming of Montero had left him overconfident, but Montero was as surprised as anyone when his blade not only found an opening in Diego's defense but went on to nick him in the side, just above the waist. Had Montero not taken a moment to gloat, he might have been able to end the fight then and there, but a moment was all de la Vega needed to spin out of harm's way. Montero slashed savagely at him, nevertheless, his errant strokes knocking two lighted torches from their sconces.

Diego contrived his parries and ripostes to bring himself *corp-a-corp* with Montero—body to body—at which point he suddenly took hold of Montero's sword arm and sent it smashing backwards into the wall, once more divesting him of his weapon. At the same time, Diego's own blade rose to meet Montero's throat.

"We seem to be right back where we started earlier this evening, Comandante," he said in a taunting voice, despite the flintlocks aimed at him. "Remember your orders," he called over his shoulder to the soldiers. "This fight is between us."

Montero trembled with rage. "Yes—between de la Vega and *all* of us!"

Hammers cocked. Desperate to intercede, Esperanza rushed forward once more, just as the loud report of a musket sounded and the sulfurous smell of inferior grade gunpowder filled the room. A momentary silence fell over everyone. Both Montero and Diego turned to see Esperanza stumble and collapse, a red blemish blossoming on the bodice of her silk gown.

Stunned, Diego let the sword drop from his hand and hastened to his wife's side, lifting her by the shoulders and calling her name. Morning Dove's anguished wail escaped the hand of the solider who had hold of her.

"No," Diego uttered. "No!"

His back still pressed to the wall, Montero slowly lowered himself and took up the sword; then, descending a few steps, he plunged it straight into the heart of the troop who held the smoking gun. The rest of the soldiers grew edgy, but to a man they silently submitted to Montero's glowering survey.

The smell of smoke roused Montero from confused dismay. The torches he'd inadvertently toppled had set fire to a tapestry, and flames were already climbing toward the foyer's high ceiling. Without thinking, he raced up the stairs to where Diego knelt, cradling Esperanza's lifeless body.

"I'm sorry," he blurted. "I would never have let any harm come to her."

Diego's eyes were animated by a cold fury when he looked up. "She was never yours to protect."

He might have said more had Elena's cries not reached him; then he became aware of the smoke that was rapidly filling the house, and he grew alarmed. Laying Esperanza gently to the floor, he rose stiffly and managed one step toward the infant's room before Montero swung the sabre's handguard into the back of his head.

Diego fell, hard, to the floor. Quickly, a soldier moved in with an unsheathed knife, but Montero put out a restraining arm. "No, let him live." He leaned over Diego, who groaned slightly. "I have better plans for him."

Montero moved to Esperanza. Anguish and disbelief welled up in him at the sight of her inert body. Trembling as he knelt beside her, he reached down and closed her eyes.

The world faded in and out of focus as Diego struggled to climb from the black pit of unconsciousness. For a moment he knew only that he was outdoors, lying on his side, and that he couldn't straighten his legs. Gradually he realized that two of

Montero's soldiers were standing nearby. Bringing his hands to his face, he saw, too, that his wrists were shackled. Confused, he forced his eyes to obey his will.

He soon grasped that he was trapped in an iron cage set atop a rickety *carreta*—an oxcart. The fire brightening the raven night was his house, engulfed in flames. Fragments of the duel on the staircase burst into his mind; then the dreadful sight of the life going out of Esperanza's eyes, the mournful sound of the infant's cries—

"Elena!" he shouted. "Elena!"

Flames licked higher into the night sky, illuminating several skittish horses and their riders—Montero's troops, along with some of the hacienda's *vaqueros*. Diego thought he heard Morning Dove, screaming something indecipherable. Then, all at once, he discerned a figure dashing from the burning house—Montero! And in his arms he held a small bundle wrapped in blankets and cloth.

Diego pulled himself upright and watched as his archenemy approached the cage, his face black with smoke, a bloody bandage dangling from his neck. Diego's anguish yielded to momentary relief, then elation when he heard Elena wailing. He thrust his hands between the iron bars, as far as the shackles permitted.

"Montero! Give her to me! Let me hold her!"

Montero stopped just out of reach, rocking Elena in his arms and comforting her with gentle pats on the back. "There, there, little one, you're safe now. Nothing to fret about. No harm will come to you. Yes, that's it, stop crying and smile for me." He turned the infant so that Diego could see her. "Ah, it's true what they say: you do have your mother's eyes."

Diego gripped the rusty bars and shook the cage so hard it began to wobble on the cart. "You can't imprison me—you haven't the authority!"

Sudden blood mottled Montero's face. "Who said anything about authority, de la Vega? As I told you: this is just between the two of us."

Diego laughed madly. "Then go ahead and cart me off to jail. I'll be set free the moment Santa Anna's troops arrive. And as God is my witness, Montero, no frigate or brigantine will keep you from my reach. I'll track you to the ends of the earth."

"At one time, I would have taken that threat seriously," Montero replied in a colorless and controlled voice. "But where you're going, there'll be no one to set you free. Not until I say so, which is to say, *never*. Do you hear me, de la Vega—never."

Diego's eyes bulged from his head. "Then kill me now and be done with it! Kill me now, or I swear you will never be rid of me!"

"What, and rob my countrymen of the satisfaction of having you suffer for what they had to endure at the hands and blade of El Zorro?" Montero kept his voice even, purposely plunging his words, like rapier thrusts, into Diego's heart. "No, I prefer to let you live with the knowledge that you have lost everything you once held dear. To suffer as I have, watching you and Esperanza all these years, knowing that this child should have been mine."

Diego raised his gaze to the smoke-filled sky. "Damn you to hell, Montero!"

Montero made no attempt to conceal his gratification. "As I have you, de la Vega." As he turned and walked away, lightning flashed over the ocean, thunder rolled across the vast landscape, and the first heavy drops of rain spattered on the thirsty ground.

One of the soldiers leaned toward the cage. "No man survives the dungeon at Talamantes," he intoned stonily. "Not even Zorro." Turning to the wagon driver, he added, "Away with him."

A lash sounded. The wagon jerked into motion and began to roll steadily through the driving storm.

Changing of the Guard

THROUGHOUT THE 1830S, WHILE DE ITURBIDE AND then Antonio López de Santa Anna Pérez de Lebrón grappled with making the most of Mexico's hard-won independence, Alta California remained a remote land, populated by a mere 4,000 persons of Spanish or Creole descent, and perhaps 150,000 indigenous tribal peoples.

Once he became president, Santa Anna refortified the presidios and extended Alta California's northern frontier to the 42nd parallel by having a mission founded at San Francisco Solano, but he reneged on his promise to turn mission land over to the Indian neophytes who had so faithfully served the Church. Instead, he awarded huge tracts of ranch and grazing land to aristocrats and military officers who had won his favor; and in their wake followed trappers, land speculators, and Boston men, off ships that came around Cape Horn delivering quantities of satin, sugar, shoes, jewelry, tea, hardware, cotton, and calico, in exchange for California's hides, sea otter pelts, tallow, and lard.

By 1841, many Californios had begun asking themselves why Santa Anna was not only tolerant of the increase in foreign trade but encouraging of it, given the fact that foreign influence had lost him Texas and, more recently, New Mexico. All who settled in the mission towns were obliged to convert to Catholicism, but it didn't necessarily follow that the newcomers' renunciation of Protestantism guaranteed allegiance to Mexico. Many thought that it was just a matter of time before Californios began calling for independence, as had the Tejanos and the New Mexicans before them.

Rafael Montero had monitored Santa Anna's actions from afar, but with great interest. Montero was known to have traveled widely—and in extreme wealth—in Europe and throughout Central and South America. It was rumored that somewhere along the way he had taken a wife, who had died shortly after bearing him a beautiful, spirited daughter, whom he seldom permitted to be out of his sight. It was also rumored that Montero had become friendly with Santa Anna himself, and that he had accepted a commission in the Mexican Army. Mail arrived periodically in Los Angeles, addressed both to the dons he had left behind, as well as to the Mexican commandant who had replaced him. It was thought by many that scores of people were working for Montero during his protracted absence, airing out the *casa mayor* he still retained in the pueblo and keeping his political bed warm until his promised return.

Don Diego de la Vega was widely believed to have died in the hacienda fire that also claimed the lives of his wife and infant daughter, though for some time rumors circulated to the contrary. As for Zorro, he seemed to have simply disappeared into the night from which he had been born—perfidiously, to some. For a true champion of the oppressed wouldn't have turned a blind eye to the injustices perpetrated by the Mexican military. More importantly, a true champion would have returned to put an end to the mysterious disappearances that plagued the territory, from Santa Barbara to Capistrano. Up and down the Camino Real—the grand road that linked the mission towns—people whispered tales of dark riders on horseback who would appear at dusk at settlers' homesteads or Indian wickiups to spirit away entire families—to the extent that none were seen or heard from again.

As for the Murieta brothers, angered by the administrators' continued broken promises to the neophytes and the errant neglect for their distant subjects, they had turned to banditry, taking what they needed from the supply wagons and stagecoaches that plied Alta California's increasingly traveled highways. . . .

"You should be out apprehending desperados instead of helping yourselves to my meager wares," the owner of the general store berated Cadet Corporal Lopez when he plucked the choicest peach from one of the store's wooden bins. The owner was as slender as Lopez was rotund, but his seeming frailty belied an dauntless spirit.

Lopez's quick, ravenous bites made short work of the peach nevertheless. "You should be honored to have an soldier of my rank steal your fruit, *viejo,*" he said around a mouthful of juicy pulp. He reached for a second peach, but the old man beat him to it and threw it far into the chaparral.

"Better the coyotes should have it than the likes of you."

Lopez wiped his ample mouth with the back of his hand, laughed, and grabbed another peach before the old man could stop him.

The dilapidated store was situated alongside a water station on a secondary road that ran between Los Angeles and San Pedro harbor. Some of Lopez's half-dozen underlings were seeing to the team of horses that pulled their wagon, while others were sating themselves on tomatoes or melons, or filling their pockets with olives, lentils, garbanzos, or chilis. They wore uniforms of dusty, threadbare dark blue serge, accented with red piping and white crossbelts, and tall shakos made of dull black leather, with chinstraps and cockade loops. One soldier sat atop a wooden strongbox in the back of the wagon, a walnut-stocked Brown Bess flintlock laid over his lap.

"Bandits prowl the territory, and all you do is graze, like cattle," the proprietor muttered. His crooked finger indicated a sepia reward poster nailed to the store's front wall. "These two. Why aren't you off chasing these two?"

Lopez glanced at the *gratificación* notice, which depicted the faces of two men of about thirty years. One was thickly bearded and fine-featured; the other, lean and crafty-looking. A printed legend below the drawings read: WANTED FOR THIEVERY AND ASSORTED ACTS OF MAYHEM: JOAQUIN AND ALEJANDRO MURIETA.

Lopez was about to comment when a young boy skulked from the store, as if fearful of a beating. Lopez studied him for a moment, then extended the peach in offering, but the youth failed to so much as acknowledge him.

41

"What's wrong with him?" Lopez asked the proprietor.

The old man's eyes tracked the boy for a few seconds. "He comes from a family of fishermen who lived near San Pedro. But they were disappeared some weeks ago. My wife and I have taken the boy in, but I don't think it will be long before the riders come for him." He worked his whiskered jaw. "For my wife and myself, as well."

Lopez sank his square teeth into the peach and shrugged. "Tall tales."

"More people disappear every day—ranchers, farmers, Indians." The old man grew angrier as he spoke. "And what do you do? You steal food and shrug."

The remark had barely emerged from his mouth when Lopez rose in sudden fury and struck him across the face, knocking him to the ground, where he lay still, eyeing the cadet corporal with contempt.

"President Santa Anna sent you here to watch over us, and this is how you behave to your own people?" He struggled to his feet, clapped the dust from his ragged clothes, and spit on the ground. "Alta California is worse now than it was under the Spanish Crown. Then, at least, the oppressed had Zorro to call on."

"Zorro?" Lopez sniggered. "A taller tale. And even if he did exist, he'd be no match for me." He patted his substantial gut.

"Who is Zorro?" the young boy asked, the name alone sufficient to rouse him from apprehension.

"The masked avenger of the people," the proprietor explained proudly. "One who could appear out of the blackness, slip though keyholes, ride like the wind, as if joined to his black steed—"

42

"Corporal Lopez!" one of the soldiers shouted. "Strangers."

Lopez followed the troop's finger to the road, where a man on horseback seemed to materialize out of the ambient dust and afternoon glare. Behind him shuffled two more men, yoked to each other and to the horse by a thick rope. As Lopez's soldiers moved away from the food bins and water troughs to regard the trio at closer range, the strains of a song—sung to the tune of "Camptown Races"—came to them on the dry wind.

"Caught me some bandits, plain to see, do-dah, do-dah; plenty mean, but they don't scare Three, oh, the do-dah day. Stayed right on their tracks, climbed right up their backs. So gather up the bounty due to me, 'cause . . ."

A powerful-looking man in chaps and a high-crowned sombrero, the rider cupped a hand to his ear, as if cuing his quarry to finish the verse. When the pair saw that the rider was baiting them with his canteen, they complied in unison: "'Cause nobody's tough as Jack. Yeah, nobody's tough as Jack.'"

Jack tipped the contents of the canteen over his trail-dusted face, then tossed it to the leaner of the captives, who in turn passed it to his bearded *compadre*. Greedily, the bearded one raised the canteen to his lips, only to find it empty.

"Sin verguenza," he snarled, hurling the canteen aside.

But Jack paid him no mind. "Hey, hey, come one, come all," he was calling out to Lopez and the others. "Come have the fright of your lives! See the notorious Murieta brothers. Horse thieves, robbers, plunderers!"

One of the soldiers glanced at the wanted poster,

43

tore it from the wall, and handed it to Lopez. "Santa Maria—the *Murietas!*" the corporal said, with a note of awe. "Big as life!" Hushed exclamations rose from the rest as Lopez stepped forward to confront the trio.

Dismounting, the bounty hunter asked to have a look at the poster. His left hand sported only three fingers. A makeshift tin prosthesis was strapped on to where his fourth and fifth fingers used to be. Around one metal finger was an elaborate turquoise ring. And jutting from the band of his hat were what appeared to be the bleached bones of the missing digits.

"These men are now in the custody of the military," Lopez announced. "We'll take them the rest of the way to Los Angeles." He looked Jack up and down. "You can claim your bounty at the *cuartel general.*"

Jack laughed derisively. "Yeah, when bears start wearin' dresses." Unscrewing the tip of his aluminum pinky, he withdrew a match from inside.

"So how much we worth?" the bearded captive asked.

Striking the match on his prosthesis, Jack lit up a cigarillo. His response was almost apologetic. "All figured, Alejandro, about two hundred pesos."

Alejandro traded astonished looks with his brother, Joaquin, from whose neck hung some sort of silver coin or medallion that glinted in the harsh sunlight. "That's it?" Joaquin said. "A lousy two hundred pesos apiece?"

"Enough of this," Lopez started to say.

"Uh, the two hundred's for the both of you," Jack went on. " 'Course, you have to realize, what with the local magistrates being a bit hollow-pocketed just now on account of their spending on whores and gaming, that cash rewards for bloodthirsty desperados such as yourselves are way down all over the territory."

44

Lopez growled. "Enough talking—"

"Don't accept it, Jack," Alejandro said. "Not after working so hard to bring us in. You can probably get more for us in Monterey or Santa Barbara."

Lopez took a menacing step forward and slapped Alejandro hard across the face. "I told you to shut up!"

But no sooner had the words left his mouth than Joaquin drew a pistol, as if from thin air, and aimed it at Lopez's head. "Touch my brother again and you die here and now," he said in a voice as hard and cold as his eyes.

Lopez staggered back, raising his plump hands. "Aye, I thought you were roped up?"

Joaquin grinned at him. "As you were meant to, *gordito.*"

Lopez's eyes darted; then, with surprising agility for his girth, he flung himself to one side, shouting, "Take them!"

Joaquin fired the pistol, but the shot went wide. Spooked, the horse reared up, nearly strangling both Joaquin and Alejandro, but Three-Fingered Jack regained control of the beast before the soldiers were upon them.

Alejandro dropped to his knees as two soldiers rushed forward. Again, the yoking rope went taut, causing Joaquin to drop the pistol. But tensed, the rope provided a neat snag for the soldiers, who struck it face-first and fell to the ground. Quickly, Alejandro slipped the loop from his neck and threw himself at the pair, subduing one with well-timed punches and the other with a swift kick to the face.

On the run, a third soldier was already taking aim at Alejandro, but Joaquin managed to knock the rifle aside with a tarnished spadroon he drew from its place of concealment in the bedroll on Three-Fingered Jack's horse.

"Damn it, brother," Joaquin shouted, rubbing his rope-burned neck. "Warn me next time!"

The soldier lunged with his bayonet, casting the ancient sword from Joaquin's hands, but Joaquin succeeded in yanking the musket from the soldier's grip. Swinging it like a club, he caught the soldier on the side of his face, dropping him; he then raised the gun to his shoulder to discourage further attacks from any of the others.

Lopez, meanwhile, found himself staring down the barrel of Three-Fingered Jack's sawed-off Bess. "Reckon this ought to raise the reward some, eh, Corporal?" Three-Finger said with a grin.

"Sin verguenza," Lopez remarked through gritted teeth.

Alejandro laughed and motioned with his chin to the strongbox. "Until then, we'll just have to make do with the *plata* you're carrying." Moving for the box, he caught the eye of the proprietor, who almost smiled.

"Fetch the boys some water and some fruit," the old man told the boy at his side.

Three-Fingered Jack stood glaring at Lopez. "Y'know what chafes me most about this poster—more than the measly two hundred pesos? That it don't even mention *me!*" He glanced at Alejandro and Joaquin. "Ain't I the one figgered how to kidnap the mayor out of his own outhouse?" Without warning, he grabbed Lopez by the lapels of his jacket. "I'm the holy guts of this gang, y'understand? Without Three-Fingered Jack, the whole damn opera falls apart!"

Desperados

*T*HE THREE BANDITS HADN'T GONE MORE THAN THREE leagues in the stolen wagon when the ocean came into view and the road began to twist down through hedgehog cactus and coastal sage toward San Pedro harbor. Joaquin was driving, and Alejandro rode in back, with the strongbox. Three-Fingered Jack's horse was tied to the rear of the wagon, and Jack himself was in the shotgun seat. Born in Santa Fe, Jack's real name was Manuel Garcia. He had thrown in with the Murietas four years earlier in Mazatlan, where Joaquin and Alejandro were lying low after a string of daring robberies in Baja California.

"So what're you planning to do with your share of the loot?" Jack asked Joaquin.

Joaquin didn't have to think about it. "Buy myself a saddle with a silver pommel and parade through the streets of San Diego on the finest beast I can find—an Appaloosa, maybe. People will see me and say, 'Now, there rides a wealthy caballero.' What about you?"

47

"Actually, I've been thinking of headin' on up to Monterey or Yerba Buena for a spell," Jack said. "Buy myself a beautiful woman, and spend my days sipping *amontillado,* playing *monte,* and smoking cigars."

Joaquin laughed. "You mean you're tired of living on beef jerky and *frijoles, hombre?*" He glanced over his shoulder at Alejandro. "And you, little brother?"

Alejandro snorted in playful derision. "My dreams are no match for the likes of yours or Jack's."

Joaquin winked at Jack and clapped his brother on the shoulder. "Come now, *'mano,* tell us again about the cattle ranch and the love of a sweet señorita who'll bear you a dozen children. . . ."

Alejandro took the ribbing good-naturedly. "Better love than a fancy saddle or a couple of drunk nights in Monterey," he said after a moment. "Real dreams are wasted on you two."

The three of them spent a few minutes laughing at the ease with which they had outwitted the soldiers, whom they'd left buck naked and roped together in a circle around a tall barrel cactus. Then Alejandro turned his attention to the locked strongbox. Despite the rust that had accumulated on the lock, it had refused to yield to repeated blows from the butt of one of the stolen muskets; so now, with Jack looking on, Alejandro simply trained the business end of the gun on the lock and blew it open, the report of the shot echoing in the coastal hills.

Lifting the lid, he expected to find leather pouches of gold and silver coins, but, in fact, the box contained nothing more than a single rat—rightfully panicked and probably deaf from the rifle round—who skittered up Alejandro's arm before leaping from the wagon into the underbrush.

"We've been set up!" he yelled over the noise of the jouncing wagon.

Joaquin pulled the horses up short alongside a steep ravine. Alejandro had his mouth open to explain what he'd found when he spied, through the dust of their sudden stop, six mounted soldiers spanning the road some distance ahead. A glance back at the way they had come revealed half-a-dozen others positioned on the ridgeline.

Joaquin looked from one group to the other. "Why are they just sitting there when they have us hemmed in? They're not even drawing a bead on us."

"Maybe they mean to take us alive," Alejandro suggested.

"Fat chance of that," Jack countered, already priming the Brown Bess they'd taken from Lopez's guard.

Joaquin eyed the ravine. "We're not hemmed in."

Jack surveyed the steep incline and nodded glumly. "I take your meaning, *compadre.*"

Without another word, the three hurled themselves out of the wagon and down the slope, running at first, then tumbling out of control and raising huge dust devils that might have been visible clear to San Pedro. His sabre in hand, Alejandro hit the bottomland almost at the same moment as Joaquin, and nearly on top of his brother. Jack, off to one side, was sliding rapidly toward an even steeper drop. As he went hurtling over the edge, Alejandro heard him scream in pain. An instant later the report of a pistol reached his ears.

Alejandro picked himself up off the ground and scurried to a better vantage, where he saw Jack, bleeding from his right thigh, sprawled below a blond, mounted soldier in the dark blue buttoned uniform of a cavalry officer—a Yankee, by the look of him—with

49

a Paterson Navy Colt revolver aimed more or less at Jack's heart. Behind the Yankee ranged a group of mounted lancers, wearing chaps, serapes, and tall sombreros, all carrying lassos in addition to their iron-tipped *yarrochas.*

Joaquin moved alongside Alejandro and shoved him into motion, while he scooted off in the opposite direction. Alejandro hadn't gone fifty meters when he heard a second shot ring out. Turning, he saw Joaquin on the ground, holding his leg, and the Yankee calmly lowering a rifle from his shoulder. Ignoring his brother's appeals that he keep moving, Alejandro hurried to his side and began to drag him toward a cluster of scrub oak, halfway up the incline.

"It's useless, Alejandro," Joaquin protested. "Leave me."

Alejandro shook his head. "I won't. As you wouldn't leave me."

After repeated backslides, however, Joaquin drew his pistol from his cummerbund and thrust it under Alejandro's chin. *"Vayate*—now!"

Alejandro recognized it as more of a plea than a threat, and finally nodded. "I'll find a way to free you, brother."

Joaquin grinned. "Hurry, Alejandro."

Alejandro dug the toes of his boots into the sandy soil and sprinted for the cover of the stunted brush, even as the Yankee and the lancers were closing in on Joaquin.

Seated imperially on his mount, Harrison Love ordered one of the lancers to gag and hog-tie Three-Fingered Jack, who was wincing in pain from the round that had shattered his upper leg bone; he then trotted his horse toward where Joaquin lay bleeding.

The rest of the lancers formed a circle around the bandit, their red-pennoned, wooden-shafted spears pointed inward. They made room for Love, who came to a halt alongside Murieta, his sabre drawn and dangling at his side.

A former captain in Sam Houston's Texas army and one of the men who had been chosen to escort the captured Santa Anna back across the Rio Grande, Love combined the refined bearing of a career officer with the grizzled look of a frontiersman. On the ride to Mexico, he and Santa Anna had spent countless hours talking, soldier to soldier, and by the time they had reached Saltillo, they had become friends. It was Santa Anna who introduced him to several influential Californios, who had ultimately convinced Love that men of initiative could make easy fortunes in the West.

"What do you want with me?" Murieta asked Love when he could.

Love smoothed the ends of his thick moustache. "Just trying to clean up the territory, *hombre.*"

"Then you can start by going back to Texas or wherever you came from."

Love laughed pleasantly. "The name's Harrison Love. And I want you to know that I consider it a genuine honor to arrest you in the name of the Mexican government."

"Arrest me? You're a damn Yankee!"

"And you're the bandit Joaquin Murieta," Love answered coolly. "Wanted for sundry acts of thievery, from Monterey to Todos Santos."

"It's true that I'm Joaquin Murieta," the wounded man answered through obvious pain, "but I'm no bandit. The name is a common one throughout Alta California, and you have me confused with someone else."

51

Love smiled without showing his teeth. "You know, Joaquin, you might be right about that. But seein' as how I'm not carrying any sketches of the bandit Murieta that I could compare to your face, I reckon I'm just gonna have to carry your face and compare it to the drawings when I have the opportunity." He tapped the sabre against his leg and cut his eyes toward one of the lancers. "Prop him up."

The lancer dismounted and forced Murieta into a sitting position. Love had his blade raised to strike when the bandit spit in the face of the lancer, drew a pistol from beneath his body, and shot himself point-blank in the heart. Spattered with blood, the lancers recoiled in shock and indignation. Only Love sat unmoving on his horse.

"I'll have your head in any case," he said after a moment.

Raising the sword once more, he swung it through a swift arc, decapitating Murieta with one stroke. The silver medallion Joaquin had worn since childhood, a gift from the noblest of all Alta California's renegades, flew from his severed neck, but Love ignored it.

"Find the brother," he ordered some of the lancers while he was wiping Murieta's blood from the blade. "And somebody sling Three-Fingered Jack over a horse."

"And this one?" one of the lancers asked, pointing to the headless corpse without looking at it. "What do you want done with him?"

Love slid the sabre into its scabbard. "Bury the body but bag the head—for identification purposes."

Alejandro ground his teeth to keep from screaming and revealing his whereabouts to the lancers who were moving through the brush, poking their weapons at random into the dense thickets. The slash of the Yankee's sabre and the sight of Joaquin's spurting blood repeated themselves endlessly in his mind. He could only pray that Joaquin was already dead when the blade met his flesh.

He conjured a memory of the Yankee's broad, whiskered face. Harrison Love, he had called himself. But what was a Yankee doing riding with Mexican lancers—unless he had been hired by the territorial governor? Now even the rumor of the payroll shipment had the stink of the Yankee. All of it had been engineered to lure the Murietas and Three-Fingered Jack from hiding.

The lancers were being halfhearted in their search; if any of them had been trackers, they would have already discovered him. Alejandro hunkered down and waited for nightfall.

By dusk the soldiers had given up the search. He picked his way down to the floor of the ravine and retraced his steps to where he and Joaquin had separated. There a small pool of blood, black in the moonlight, had yet to be absorbed by the soil. Alejandro considered exhuming Joaquin from the shallow grave the lancers had dug, but he knew that he wouldn't be able to look upon his brother's headless body.

Instead, he satisfied himself by saying a prayer— that Joaquin find forgiveness in Heaven, and that he, Alejandro, live long enough to avenge Joaquin's death.

He was crossing himself when his gaze was drawn to a gleaming in the moonlight among the small stones nearby. On hands and knees he advanced towards the source of the reflection, and in a moment he had plucked Joaquin's medallion from the ground—the one Zorro had given them twenty years earlier. The feel of it was enough to wrench an anguished moan from deep within him. Clenching his hand around the engraved circle, he hunched over Joaquin's grave and gave loud voice to the grief bottled inside him.

Recalled to Life

ANCHORED OFF THE COAST, JUST SOUTH OF SANTA Barbara, the brigantine *Ayacucho* rocked in the waves of the moonlit Pacific. Built in Guayaquil and captained by a Scotsman, she was three hundred tons of meticulous craftsmanship, with tall, raking masts and stiff, square yards. From her portside rail, Rafael Montero gazed at the dark land, marveling at the fact that two decades had passed since he'd last set eyes on California, his home more than anywhere else in the world.

"Don Montero, the quarter boat is ready," the brig's captain was saying. "But I feel obliged to caution you once more about undertaking such a landing at night. These waters can be treacherous at this time of year—even for the best of my hands. So why not wait till morning and debark at San Pedro with the rest of the passengers?"

Montero turned to him, drawing back the hood of his cloak. Captain Simpson was a well-meaning man of fifty years, but Montero hadn't sailed all the way from Brazil to be deterred by some rough surf. "Your concern for my safety is most appreciated, Captain. But there is something I need to attend to this evening—while there's still time."

"Time for what, sir—if you don't mind my asking?"

"Time to ensure that nothing untoward will stand in the way of my homecoming."

Four sailors in checkered shirts, duck trousers, and varnished caps rowed Montero ashore, keeping the quarter boat stern-on to the swells. Just short of the shore, two of the tars—burly men from the Sandwich Islands—threw themselves over the gunwales into the pounding combers to help run the boat high and dry onto a rocky stretch of beach. By the flicker of torches, Montero could see a rangy figure waiting with two horses.

The dark figure approached from the shadows as Montero was being helped from the boat. "Welcome back to California, Don Montero."

Montero shook the proffered hand. "Good to see you again, Captain Love." He appraised the Texan for a moment. "It appears that California has not been unkind to you."

"Kinder than Mexico City was, sir. Excepting our meeting there, of course."

"Of course." Montero instructed the four sailors to await his return, then he mounted the spare horse. "You can tell me of all you've been doing while we ride, Captain Love. I want to be back here long before sunrise."

Love threw himself into his saddle. From the pommel hung a burlap sack, bulging with something that approximated the size of a human head. "That

56

shouldn't be a problem, sir. California's byways are a lot safer now than they used to be."

Talamantes Prison lay only two hours away by a recently blazed trail that followed the coast, linking Santa Barbara to San Pedro. Unlike the penal colony at Todos Santos in Baja California, Talamantes had always been reserved for the territory's lowborn incorrigibles—highwaymen, cutthroats, sexual offenders, and others. A brooding rectangle of uncut stone and rotting timbers, it rose from the marshy banks of a brackish estuary that was said to poison any who entered it, let alone drank from it. Off to one side of the structure, a score of crude crosses marked what passed for the prison's cemetery.

While they rode, Montero and Love had spoken of the three years that had elapsed since their fateful meeting in Mexico, in the company of President Santa Anna. Love had spent the intervening years in Los Angeles, while Montero had visited Argentina and Peru, among other nations.

Love and Montero hitched their horses to a rail at the gated entrance and demanded of the forlorn guards stationed there that they be escorted to the warden's quarters immediately. Inside, large rats scurried through murky puddles of dripping water and anguished moans emanated from the dark bowels of the place. The lengthy streaks below pairs of wall-mounted shackles might have been rust or dried blood. A rank-smelling corridor ended at a tiny room on the ground floor, indistinguishable from the holding cells that surrounded it, save that it lacked a door of iron bars, or indeed a door of any sort.

The guard's lantern spilled scant light across the

spread-eagled body of a slovenly man of indeterminate years. On the floor alongside a sagging army cot stood an upended jug that had probably been filled with tequila or *aguardiente* at the start of the evening. Moving to a rickety table, Love took hold of a wash basin and hurled its filthy contents into the face of the supine, snoring figure.

Surfacing from demon-plagued slumber, the warden bolted upright, flailing his arms about. Gradually, his blinking eyes focused on Love, then Montero. The sight of them seemed to instill more terror than relief, however, and he groped urgently for the percussion pistol Love had already moved out of reach. "Who are you? What do you want of me?"

Montero lowered the hood of his cloak to reveal his face, which had not changed appreciably since his last visit to Talamantes in 1822, except for the considerable gray in his beard and a slightly receding hairline.

Recognizing him immediately, the warden leaped to his feet and did his best to impart order to his disheveled appearance. Mopping his dripping face with his sleeve, he attempted a salute, nearly thumbing himself in the eye in the process.

"Don Montero! Is it truly you, or am I seeing a ghost?"

A thin smile spread across Montero's face. "It's me in the flesh, Sergeant Romero, rather than some figment loosed from your bottle. I sent word that you were to expect me."

"Yes, señor, of course you did. But that must have been almost three years ago. And I thought—"

"You thought what?"

"Excuse me, señor, but there is no shortage of ways for a man to come to an untimely end in this world."

58

Tucking in his shirt and straightening somewhat, Romero glanced warily at Love. "How may I be of service, señores?"

"I've come to call on one of your prisoners," Montero told him.

"Which one would that be, señor?"

"An old enemy," Montero said, more to himself. Then, emerging from a brief reverie, he took a step in Romero's direction. "His name is Diego de la Vega."

"De la Vega," the warden said, caressing a stubbled double chin in thought. "Forgive me, Don Montero, but so many come and go, I scarcely remember their names any longer. They go nameless even into the graves outside."

Montero narrowed his gaze. "He was brought here twenty years ago."

"Twenty years! Ah, but he must surely have died by now, señor."

Montero shook his head ruely. "Not de la Vega. He had good reason to go on living."

Lantern in hand, Romero escorted Montero through the prison's reeking corridors, while a guard named Ordaz brought up the rear. As they ventured deeper into Talamantes, the anguished moans became louder and more persistent. Water dripped from the stone walls like sweat from a laborer's back, and countless pairs of rodent eyes glowed in the dark.

"There are worse fates than death," Ordaz remarked.

"That, too, was what I once thought," Montero replied. "But I fear I let my emotions rule when I should have been guided by instinct."

Romero followed the conversation as he led the way

59

down a winding stone staircase. "I myself was once promised a promotion for keeping my position here. Perhaps you recall, Don Montero—"

"My sympathies that your promotion has been delayed. But I suggest you give thanks that you've had work."

Romero's forehead furrowed in annoyance, but he said nothing. Unlocking a door at the bottom of the staircase, he waved them into a narrow passageway, on which opened two long rows of iron-barred cells. Turbid water was puddled on the floor and the stench issuing from the cells was almost unbearable. Montero was excited nonetheless.

"He's here," he said through a handkerchief he held to his mouth and nose, "I can feel it."

Romero ordered Ordaz and two other guards to unlock the cells. "De la Vega, you said. A nobleman, by the sound of the name. We haven't had many of those in some time."

"He went by a second name—a name some thought carried magical power. . . ." Montero said offhandedly.

"Magical power," Romero repeated. "You must be talking about the bandit known as Zorro. It has long been rumored that he is among the prisoners here."

Montero's eyes clouded with disdain, though he allowed a nod of acknowledgment.

In a moment, two lines of shackled, emaciated prisoners stood slouching outside their cells. The sound of rough, hacking coughs punctuated the torch-lit silence. Ordaz and the guards positioned themselves at intervals along the corridor, clubs in hand. Transfixed, Montero stared at the prisoners; he then began to walk slowly down the line, scrutinizing each of the gaunt, sallow faces, and feeling as apprehensive as he had when the brigantine *Ayacucho* had been forced to negotiate the storm-tossed Strait of Magellan on the return voyage to California.

He paused before a bowed, gray-haired face, and used his gloved right hand to lift the prisoner's chin. The face that greeted him was neither more nor less haggard than those of his fellows, but the man's eyes were mere black pools. However long the man had been in Talamantes, the will had gone out of him long ago, leaving a feeble, rag-clothed shell, bearded and wild-maned. Even so, Montero thought he sensed a trace of former strength and agility, even nobility. Maybe it was the way the man's eyes suddenly seemed to harden, become more lucid, perhaps in recognition. He was about to ask the prisoner to identify himself when the warden's voice rang out.

"If the one once called Zorro is here, stand forth and show yourself. Otherwise, things will be unpleasant for all of you."

The prisoners seemed to tremble en masse, then, after a long moment, a feeble voice cried, "I'm the Fox!"

Startled, Montero swung away from the old man and moved to the one who had spoken—a shriveled man who made a pathetic show of waving one hand about, as if it were even capable of gripping a sword.

"They took away my mask, my rapier, my horse. . . ."

"Close your mouth, you stinking old troll," someone else said.

Montero's eyes settled on a tall, muscular black man.

"I'm the man you're looking for. I am Zorro."

"Lies, more lies," said another voice. "Why, anyone can see that you're too tall to be Zorro. I'm the one. I'm the one!"

Montero's face contorted in anger. He might have struck the black man had not another prisoner—ever more ancient and skeletal than the hollow-eyed one—proclaimed himself to be Zorro.

"I'm Zorro's sister," announced another, whose rotted flesh was covered with oozing sores.

Shortly, almost everyone in the dungeon was either claiming to be Zorro or arguing with others who had. The corridor seemed to close in on Montero, and the stench of the place became asphyxiating. Even de la Vega couldn't have survived twenty years of it, Montero assured himself. He had to be dead. Turning one way, then the next, he suddenly hastened for the winding staircase, the handkerchief pressed to his face.

"About that promotion, Don Montero," Sergeant Romero called after him. He glowered when the prisoners laughed at him, then slumped in a gesture that accepted defeat. Glancing at Ordaz, he shouted, "Lock them up."

Diego resignedly accepted the hard shove that sent him stumbling back into his cell, but his eyes shone with a light they hadn't contained in more than a decade. He hadn't recognized Montero until the proclamations of "Zorro! Zorro!" had summoned him from the sheltering stupor he had fallen into over the years.

Around him, everyone was still shouting the name of his alter ego, but he showed no recognition as a guard locked him into his leg manacles. Ordaz hurled one they called "the Skeleton" into an adjacent cell

62

with such viciousness that the old man crashed against the rough-cut stones of the rear wall and crumpled to the ground, his eyes staring lifelessly from his sunken skull.

Ordaz stood over the Skeleton for a moment, then pressed two grimy fingers to the man's neck. "One for the cemetery!" he called, standing up. "Someone get him out of here before his stink overpowers the stench of the rest of them!"

Marshalling his thoughts, Diego waited until the guard detail had exited the dungeon before taking careful stock of his surroundings. The cells were secured and the yelling had died down. Only Ordaz remained in the corridor, his back to Diego's cell.

Diego acted. Thrusting his hands through the bars, he locked his hands around Ordaz's throat, his fingers clawing into the soft flesh around the guard's voice-box. Ordaz tried to call out, but no sound could escape Diego's hold. While the men in nearby cages strained to see what was happening, Diego yanked Ordaz back, smashing his head once, twice, three times against the rusted bars, until Ordaz slumped to the floor, unconscious or dead. Then Diego stretched out his arm and took hold of the ring of keys Ordaz wore on his belt. Unlocking his cell door, he dragged the guard inside.

Ignoring the hushed appeals that he open the other cells, Diego concentrated on unlocking his leg restraints. One by one, he tried the other keys on Ordaz's ring, but none of them served. A frantic search of the guard's pockets turned up a dagger, but even that wasn't sufficient to pry open the manacle. Then Diego spied the powder horn on Ordaz's belt. The desperateness of the plan that came to him gave him no pause. Ripping the horn away, he removed its corncob stopper and he began to fill the manacle keyhole with black powder, tamping it down with the tip of the dagger. Next, he made use of a strip of Ordaz's serge jacket as wadding. Cutting additional strips from the jacket, he wrapped them about his foot, in the hope that the twilled fabric might offer some minimal protection. Then, taking two flints from Ordaz's cartridge belt, he began to strike them against one another, raising sparks that eventually conjured drifts of smoke from the wadding.

Cupping his hands around the smoldering cloth, Diego blew gently, giving slow birth to a flame that burned quickly down the makeshift fuse. Diego leaned away from his own foot, then dragged Ordaz's body between him and the manacle to shield himself further.

A cacophony of raised voices and bar-rattling helped to mask the sound of the muffled explosion. Diego shoved Ordaz aside and wincing, pulled the burning serge wrappings from a now blackened and bloody foot. His toes were intact, however, and the manacle was open, missing a hunk of itself. A glance at Ordaz revealed the missing piece jutting from the man's chest. Diego's gaze moved to the guard's jackboots, just as the sound of footfalls could be heard on the dungeon stairway.

For the first several years of his imprisonment, Diego had kept his sanity by imagining the vengeance he would ultimately exact on Montero. The interminable days of dark, dank confinement would find him lost in extended fantasies in which he escaped Talamantes, picked up Montero's trail, and tracked him clear around the world. From California to Acapulco, and on to Lima and Santiago; then around Cape Horn to ports of call in Brazil and the Canaries; and from there to Lisboa, in Portugal. From Lisboa, it would be overland to Spain, to Madrid first, then on to Extremadura, where Montero's family had vast holdings. There he would find his archenemy, and there he would wait until he could meet him alone. Diego would grant him the dignity of dying by the sword. Then he would return to the New World, and begin again in some obscure pueblo in New Mexico or in the far north of Alta California. . . .

In those reveries, Elena always remained the child Montero had carried from the burning house. And when, after some time, Diego finally allowed himself to think of her as a young girl, then an adolescent, he would see Esperanza.

As the years passed, fewer and fewer prisoners came to Talamantes—bandits, murderers, horse thieves—and with them came news of the growth of Los Angeles under Mexican rule; of the Boston men who could be found operating lumber mills or supply stores in each of California's dozen or so settlements; of improvements to the road to Ensenada and the arrival of fur trappers from across the Sierra Madre; and of the great ships—the commercial frigates, galleons, and brigs—that arrived monthly from China, the United States, and Europe. But never was there any definite word of Montero. Or of Elena.

For a time, the lack of news only increased Diego's appetite for revenge. Each night, when the guards retired, he would charcoal concentric circles on the floor of his small cell, recreating the fencing exercises Kendall had taught him decades earlier in Madrid. With an imaginary rapier or shortsword in hand, he would work through feints and lunges, thrusts and parries, ballestras and envelopments. But then, after an attempted breakout, he and several others had been moved to the dungeon and shackled, where he could only enact the drills in his head.

He lost track of the days and weeks, but through it all he remained vigilant, calculating escape and revenge, and nurturing the memory of his wife and daughter. Deep down, the core of his being was protected. As frail as his body grew, as ill as his health became, the Diego de la Vega who had been imprisoned on that stormy night twenty years earlier survived.

And now he was meant to have his freedom—fittingly by exiting as one of the dead. . . .

By then, the guards were through the door at the bottom of the stairs. One carried a large canvas sack over his shoulder. Moments short of their arrival, Diego had staggered into the Skeleton's cell and dragged the corpse of the old man into his own cell. Then he had taken the Skeleton's place on the floor.

Lying as still as death, he allowed the guards to manhandle him into the sack. His only fear was that they would see the bodies in his own cell, or that they would notice Ordaz's boots, which lay flattened inside the waistband of Diego's tattered pants. But the other prisoners, now eager to abet his escape, were raising such a commotion that the guards were impatient to leave as quickly as possible. The black man, Suarez, had been entrusted with Ordaz's ring of keys.

Diego felt himself lifted and carried through the door and up the winding stairway; then into the cool air of an evening that had never smelled so sweet and fragrant. It was if he could inhale the whole of California with each shallow breath; and his elation at being free of Talamantes was so immense that he thought he would cry out and be discovered. But he managed to suppress his joyous sobs and retreat to that familiar place within himself, as he was laid into the earth and dirt was shoveled onto him.

The guards worked with haste. Given the depth of the hole they had dug, they might as well have left him out for the coyotes, pumas, and bears to dispose of. His lungs depleted, Diego waited until he was confident that the guards had returned to the prison. Then he drew the dagger and ripped a large opening in the bag. Dirt smelling strongly of human waste fell upon him, but he angled his body up as the dirt fell into his eyes and ears, emerging at last into moonlight, as if from a cocoon, gasping for air like a newborn. And almost at once the timeless reveries about Montero began to fill his mind. Now he wasn't even going to have to chase him halfway around the world.

Homecoming

 S WORDS GLITTERED AND CLASHED IN THE SCANT light that filtered into the cargo spaces of the *Ayacucho*, anchored in eleven fathoms, three miles out from San Pedro, safely beyond the swells of crashing surf. Armed with rapiers, a grizzled but spry old salt named LeFarge and a long-haired youth circled one another warily. Around them, stacked upon the dunnage, were crates filled with trade goods that were soon to be transported to the beach.

Rumored to have crewed on countless pirate vessels, LeFarge was summarily adept with a blade. His ripostes were deft; his parries adroit. But for all his finesse, he was no match for his slender, graceful opponent. A feint, then a lunge, and his sword was enveloped and flung aside. The tip of the other sword was poised directly at his heart.

"I'll give you this much, youngster, you've got a knack for the blade," he said in a tone that mixed admiration with the shame of defeat.

Elena Montero, dressed in men's trousers and a

ruffled shirt—the outfit she had sported for most of the trip north from South America—tipped her blade forward in salute. "My father is an expert swordsman."

"Then why come to a former sea wolf for your practice sessions, girl?"

The corners of Elena's bow-shaped mouth dropped. "My father feels that it's *improper* for a lady to learn the sword. He's a very formal man, you see. In fact, I sometimes fear that he failed to get the daughter he deserves."

"Aye, but you're a right beauty, girl," LeFarge said.

Elena flushed at the frankness of his gaze. She had her blade raised to engage LeFarge in another contest when a hatch in the deck opened, filling the below-decks space with golden light. "Elena!" someone shouted.

Her dark eyes widened. "Father!"

She traded worried glances with the sailor as a second voice, that of Captain Simpson, was heard. "I can't imagine what she'd be doing in the hold, Don Montero."

"Nor can I. But we've searched the entire ship. Where else could she be? Elena!" Montero called down the hatch again.

Elena made a quick decision. Tossing her rapier to the old man, she scooped up her traveling cape and hoisted herself up to a starboard porthole. "You fight well, LeFarge," she whispered before squirming through the small opening.

And not a moment too soon. Having stashed the two swords, the former buccaneer was pretending to check the cargo when Captain Simpson came down the ladder.

69

"LeFarge, have you seen hide or hair of Don Montero's daughter?"

"What, down here, Captain—among old tars like meself and the biggest rats this side of Valparaiso?"

"He's correct, Captain," Montero remarked from the top of the ladder. "Elena has spirit, but she's too refined for the likes of this place."

Bewildered, and beginning to fear that Elena had gone overboard, Montero followed Captain Simpson to the main deck. He was about to give utterance to his worst misgivings when Elena seemed to appear out of nowhere, wrapped in her traveling cloak.

"Where were you?" Montero asked in exasperated relief.

"Why, just there, on the quarter deck. I was watching for whales like the ones we saw off Monterey."

Montero and Simpson exchanged glances. "But we looked for you there."

Elena laughed. "Well, Father, where else could I have gone?"

Montero forgot his anger and led her to the rail. "San Pedro harbor," he said, gesturing across waves that marched like well-trained soldiers to the distant beach. "And not far inland is Los Angeles. Our new home."

Elena slipped her arm through Montero's and rested her head on his shoulder. "Monterey was exciting. But all my life, it seems, I've dreamed of coming to Los Angeles. And now that we're here, it still feels like a dream."

"Don Montero, Señorita Montero, the longboat is waiting," Simpson interrupted. "It happens that quite a crowd has assembled to welcome you ashore."

Montero squinted at the shore. "Lend me your telescope, if you would, Captain?"

Montero pointed the brass device at the beach, focused it, then handed it to Elena. "You see, daughter. Scarcely a dream."

Below the cliffs that rose above San Pedro's treeless and inhospitable beach, a makeshift market had been set up by merchants who shipped aboard the *Ayacucho* from the United States and Central America. In stalls erected in the sand, linens, kettles, fireworks, hardware, and spices were being sold or traded for quantities of pig fat or partially cured hides that had been carried over the precipices and stacked like lumber on the beach. Women dressed in their finest skirts, petticoats, and mantillas had come from Los Angeles to shop. An orchestra comprised of guitars, trumpets, violins, and accordions was tuning up, lending a festive air to the scene.

Montero stepped from the beached longboat and extended a helping hand to Elena. His welcome party of caballeros were turned out in traditional formal wear of fitted trousers with flared bottoms, ruffled cotton shirts, cummerbunds, and broad-brimmed hats with figured bands around the crowns.

"The governor has returned!" Don Luiz said.

The announcement elicited scattered applause from an unenthusiastic crowd of peons gathered behind the dons. Luiz hurried down the beach to meet Montero.

"Welcome home, Rafael," he said. "It has been too long."

Montero embraced his friend warmly, then stood back to appraise him. "Some gray in the beard, a few lines in the face, but otherwise unchanged all these years."

"Twenty years ago, I was a foolish man," Luiz said

quietly. "You said that you had favored me above all, but I saw only the surface of the truth. I had not yet learned to look *underneath*." He slipped a small pouch into Montero's hand. "Consider this an apology for my having ever doubted you."

Opening the pouch, Montero found a nugget of gold half the size of his fist. Luiz clapped him heartily on the back. "Come, Rafael. Your admirers await you."

With a wave of Luiz's hand, the orchestra commenced a triumphant-sounding tune. Montero exchanged *abrazos* and handclasps with the rest of the dons before gesturing to quiet the forced applause of the crowd. "Please, please, I know full well that all this gaiety at my homecoming is a pretense. So let's stop the show, shall we?"

An abashed silence fell over the dons and the members of the crowd. "Would it help if we chanted 'Viva Don Montero!'?" a peasant woman suggested with obvious sarcasm.

The remark drew a chorus of raucous laughter, along with the very chant suggested—though more as a taunt. The dons grew livid, but Montero took the gentle mocking in stride, smiling in a relaxed way, as if the chanting was simply part of the plan.

"Continue," he said when the voices had abated somewhat, "for you have every right to laugh. I wager that you've been paid—even threatened—to stand in the hot sun and greet me."

"No, no, Rafael," Luiz sputtered. "You have it all wrong. They *wanted* to come. These good people still have the greatest respect for you—"

"Enough flattery," Montero interrupted. "They have little reason to respect me." He turned to the peons. "And let me say this to you: I sympathize with

72

your feelings." He began to walk among them, exuding noblesse oblige and avuncular charm. "After all, why should you care about any of your leaders, past or present? The Mexican government ignores you. The dons, well, they seem content merely to cheat you. And what have any of us ever given you in return— you, who are the backbone of this territory as much as is the Sierra Madre? Who, may I ask, has ever helped you?"

"Zorro!" someone shouted. "Zorro defended us."

Blanching slightly but recovering quickly, Montero swung to the voice, then smiled. "Father Felipe, is it not? Ah, but you, too, wear a look of discontent. The missions are having a rough time of it, are they? The administrators were supposed to have turned their lands over to the neophytes and the people, and instead they grant the lands to their favorite generals and courtiers. What's more, I hear that members of your cherished flocks are disappearing in front of your eyes. And yet Zorro is nowhere to be found. Your masked defender hasn't shown himself in twenty years."

Montero spread his hands and turned a slow circle. "False hope and broken promises are all that any of you have had since I left California. Hope once offered by a bandit who hid his face behind a black mask and later deserted you, and empty promises from a womanizing aristocrat who will soon proclaim himself *dictator* of Mexico. One who has proclaimed far and wide that 'Despotism is the proper government for the Mexican people.' But I say that the time has come to cease depending on corrupt leaders and erratic champions. I say that the time has come to take destiny into our own hands. Not as Spaniards. Not as Mexicans . . . But as *Californians!*"

Few in the crowd knew what to make of Montero's remarks. Sam Houston must have said as much to the people of Texas five years earlier, but Texas independence had been hard-fought. And what had happened at the Alamo was still etched in the memories of everyone from the Rio Grande to Monterey.

"Twenty years ago I left you to the care of Mexico," Montero went on, "and in the care of some of these same caballeros gathered here today. But now I offer you this solemn pledge: to help you fight for a free and independent California!"

Preening only moments before, the dons were stunned, as murmurs of agreement swept through the crowd. Don Hector edged closer to Montero. "With all due respect, Rafael, we'd be crushed if we threw down the gauntlet to Santa Anna."

Montero grinned slyly. "But of course," he whispered back.

Some among the crowd were applauding, though not everyone was convinced. "And what is Santa Anna likely to make of your talk of independence, Don Montero?" Father Felipe asked.

Montero turned to him. "I assure you, good padre, that Santa Anna is too busy with alleged affairs of state to concern himself with California. Opposition to his absolute authority mounts daily, and if my strategy succeeds, he will gladly relinquish control of Alta California as he did the Republic of Texas, allowing us to forge not only an independent territory but a new life for ourselves—a life free from fear, neglect, or opposition!"

Again, Father Felipe failed to be moved enough to applaud Montero's rhetoric. "I, for one, remember well your notion of freedom from oppression, Don Montero."

74

Montero made no secret of his ruefulness. "Ah, but I've changed, Father," he said. "I've changed."

Diego, dressed now in white cotton trousers and a striped serape—peasant garb he had stolen from a clothes-washing spot along the river—had been making his way meter by meter toward the front of the crowd. On his feet were Ordaz's boots and tucked into his red sash was the Talamantes guard's dagger. The fact that Diego was suddenly a free man, that he had spent the past two glorious days inhaling the aromas of jojoba and romania, that he now stood in dazzling sunshine, his beard and long hair ruffled by an obliging offshore breeze, all of these meant nothing to him. As much as he had been imprisoned within the walls of Talamantes, he was now prisoner of a single overriding obsession: to kill Rafael Montero.

Initially uncertain where to look for Montero, Diego had lurked in the shadows of the *cuartel* in the Los Angeles pueblo, eavesdropping on the conversations of the dons who arrived to pay their respects to the Mexican commandant. And shortly he had learned of the arrival of the brigantine *Ayacucho,* and the much-anticipated return of the territory's former overseer, Rafael Montero.

In contrast to the taunting peons among whom he mingled, Diego was grim-faced and determined, lost to all but the sound of Montero's voice. Diego was bewildered by all that Montero was saying about Santa Anna, the Republic of Texas, and independence. He had yet to find the opening he needed, but his desperation had reached such a fevered pitch that he was ready to throw himself from the crowd like an assassin rather than the calculating avenger he saw himself. He had passed close enough to Fray Felipe to hear him say something about Montero's notion of freedom from oppression, and was about to strike when the dons suddenly converged on Montero, unwittingly buying him a few more moments of life.

Diego searched for another angle of attack, found one as Montero emerged from the surround of dons, and drew the honed dagger. He had his arm drawn back when the voice of a young woman pierced his bloodthirsty trance.

"Father?"

Both Diego and Montero turned to the voice. It belonged to a woman perhaps twenty years old, tall and striking to behold, with long, raven hair and eyes that gleamed brighter than the blade of Diego's purloined knife. Diego was dumbfounded, stricken by the vision before him. *Esperanza!* he told himself, then quickly realized his error. But the alternative was even more frightening; made all the more searing in that he had failed to even consider that *she* would have come to think of Montero as her father, and that he would return her to California.

Elena!

Almost swooning, he watched her approach, walking straight towards him. And for one instant—his befuddled, dreamy mind, forgetting what twenty years in Talamantes had done to him—he thought that she would surely recognize him; that she would reach out and embrace him. But of course she passed by him without so much as a curious glance. To her he was just a wild-haired old peon, gone to ruin from too much *pulque* or tequila. Unbearably, she went instead straight into the waiting arms of Rafael Montero!

"Gentleman," Montero said to his highborn audience, "allow me to introduce the joy and inspiration of my life—my daughter, Elena."

In their newfound enthusiasm for Montero, a peon placed a bouquet of fragrant flowers in Elena's hands. The sight of the flowers galvanized Diego, for the last time he had seen flowers of that kind, they were tied to the crib in which the infant lay asleep. He looked at Elena, who brought the flowers to her nose, inhaling deeply. Could this be the same child? Diego asked himself. Was it possible that the young women almost within arm's reach was the same curly-haired infant he had rocked to sleep so many a night?

"What is this flower called?" Elena was asking. "Its fragrance is so familiar."

"It's called romania," Don Luiz answered for the peon. "But I don't think it could possibly be familiar to you, since it grows only in California."

Once more, Elena sniffed at the bouquet, her mind seeming to wander. Diego let the dagger slip from his hand to the sand. He saw suddenly that killing Montero was not going to be as simple as he had imagined; his thirst for revenge had grown hazy with new concerns. The man he had come to loathe was the man Elena had come to adore, and to kill him would be to deprive her of the only family she knew. Like the ghost he had become, his past and future erased, Diego turned and disappeared into the crowd.

A Fateful Encounter

*T*HE SOLE CUSTOMER IN A DINGY *PULQUERÍA* ON THE Los Angeles pueblo plaza, Alejandro banged his shot glass on the table and called for a refill. His feet ached from a night of hard walking from the coast and his heart was brimming with grief and hatred. Three days had passed since the encounter with Harrison Love and the lancers, and Alejandro was determined to be blind drunk before sunrise.

"Another *mescal*—or whatever this stuff really is."

Returning a nod of acknowledgment, the immense mestizo owner of the grog shop reached for a bottle on the warped shelf behind the counter. Below the shelves stood a row of small barrels with petcocked spigots, containing cheap wine, even cheaper beer, and *aguardiente*—firewater. The shop itself was nothing more than an unlighted ramshackle hut, though it did enjoy a clear view of the square, where native vendors had their wares spread on straw mats and colorful wool blankets.

"I want you to keep this glass full," Alejandro

slurred as the owner approached. "I don't want to see bottom until that worm is swimming in my glass." He gestured to the bottle.

The owner wagged his head, around which was knotted a red bandanna. His tight-fitting, knee-length britches were blotted with wine stains and his sandals had been fashioned from palm fiber. *"Cierto, amigo,"* he told Alejandro. "But let's see some money first."

Scowling, Alejandro dug into one of his pockets but came up empty. The owner snorted and was already moving toward the counter when Alejandro's hand closed on Joaquin's medallion, which he'd slipped around his neck. "How much will this buy?" he asked, grabbing hold of the owner's arm.

The man spent a moment appraising the medallion. *"Es plata?"*

"Of course it's silver. The finest silver. All the way from . . . Zacatecas. Isn't it obvious?"

The mestizo considered it, then gave a slow nod and refilled Alejandro's glass. He was reaching for the medallion when an aged hand closed tightly around the silver piece.

Alejandro and the barkeep turned to find a tall, wild-eyed old man standing over them. Dressed in peon's clothes and jackboots, leaning on a gnarled stick that served as a cane, he looked as if he hadn't seen a bath or a square meal in some time.

"What do you want here, *viejo?"* the mestizo asked.

"Leave us," the old one said, in a quiet but firm manner that left little room for argument.

The barkeep considered it, then bit back whatever he had in mind to say. As bleary-eyed as he was, Alejandro saw something in the steely eyes of the old man that dissuaded the mestizo from making an issue of it.

"Where did you get this?" the old man demanded of Alejandro when the barkeep had walked off.

Alejandro looked him up and down, sipping from his glass.

"I asked where you got this?" the man repeated, harsher this time.

Alejandro threw the rest of the drink down in a single gulp and wiped his mouth on his sleeve. "I don't know that it's any of your business, old-timer, but it belonged to my brother. My late brother."

The man blinked and a look of sadness passed across what had once been a handsome face. "Your brother. I'm sorry to learn that he's dead."

"You're sorry?" Alejandro said bitterly. "Why should you be sorry?"

The old man ignored the question and continued to gaze longingly at the medallion, as if in memory of better times. "You shouldn't trade something so precious for a mere glass of *mescal.*"

"And why is that? You think I could get *two* glasses for it?"

Alejandro laughed at his own joke, then straightened in his chair as he saw the Texan, Harrison Love, ride into the plaza. Glaring and licking his lips, he came to his feet unsteadily, taking hold of his sabre and staggering from the table without a backward glance. He was halfway to the doorway when the old man laid a restraining hand on his shoulder.

"Who is that man to you?"

Alejandro shook off the old man's hand. "The one who murdered my brother." Again he started for the doorway, when the old man, showing surprising strength, threw him back against the *pulquería*'s wattle and daub wall.

"You're in no condition to engage a professional

soldier in swordplay. What's more, there's an old proverb that may apply: 'When you seek revenge, dig two graves; one for your enemy, one for yourself.'"

"Out of my way," Alejandro warned. "I told you before, this is none of your concern." A quick glance at the plaza, however, revealed that Love was gone. Alejandro whirled, spitting a curse. "Now I've lost him, you stupid old fool!"

The old man pressed the tip of his walking stick to Alejandro's chest. "Perhaps you'd like to demonstrate your fencing skills on me."

Alejandro's grief and frustration burst from him in a moment of uncontrolled fury. Shoving the old man back, he raised his sabre and lunged, only to find his blade deceived as the old man stepped nimbly to one side, spinning Alejandro around and sending him straight to the floor. Enraged now, he picked himself up and charged. But once more his adversary simply parried his blade, flung it from his grasp, and caught hold of it. Alejandro's momentum carried him past the old man, who whacked him with the stick, sending him into a wall and back to the floor.

"Would you care to try again?" the old man asked, looming over him.

Alejandro shook his head, defeatedly. "You're right, *viejo*. If I'm too drunk to beat you, I'm no match for anyone."

"Then, you are welcome."

"Welcome?" Alejandro got to his feet. "For what?"

"For saving your life."

Alejandro couldn't restrain a smile. "Don't give yourself too much credit. On any other day I could have killed him."

"We'll see about that. But not on this day. Your prey gives all appearances of being a trained killer,

81

where you, just now, give all appearances of being nothing more than a trained drinker. Oh, no doubt you would have fought bravely . . . but you would have been killed quickly. And who then would avenge your brother?"

Alejandro rose to his own defense. "I would have found a way. I have never lost a fight, old man."

"Ah, but you just did—to a stupid old fool with no other weapon than a blunt walking stick."

Alejandro clenched his jaw.

"If you're intent on killing this man, I can train you to do so. The correct way to move, the correct way to think. The way to take revenge with honor, and—better still—to live to celebrate it. The training will take time and dedication, of course—on my part as well as yours—but it will prove worthwhile in the end."

Alejandro stared, then shook his head in amusement. "I know I'm tipsy, but I don't remember saying that I wanted your help."

"What does that matter? As my father once told me, 'When the pupil is ready, the master will appear.'" The old man paused, then offered a bow that was not without dignity. "I am that master."

Alejandro gestured negatively. "I don't have time for that."

"Will your enemy be any less dead if you kill him a week from now? What's a month, a year, even twenty years?"

Alejandro narrowed his eyes in suspicion. "Why are you so eager to help me?"

The old man hung the medallion around Alejandro's neck. "Because you and your brother once did the same for me."

Alejandro studied the old man's face, perceiving in

his features the countenance of a man aged before his time, well ahead of his years. "Is it possible that you . . . are Zorro?"

Diego held Alejandro's incredulous gaze.

Alejandro reared back in surprise. "I—we all thought that you had disappeared, or were dead!"

"I was," Diego said after a moment.

On the grounds of the palatial hacienda Montero had purchased years earlier and kept maintained in his absence, Harrison Love and another rider were competing in an obstacle race, weaving their horses between two lines of wooden posts. Atop the posts rested large pumpkins, ripe targets for the riders' sabres.

From a safe distance, Dons Montero and Luiz, dressed in short, brocaded jackets and flat-crowned hats, watched as the stallions were spurred toward the finish line, with outstretched necks and wild, feral eyes. Montero returned his attention to a long list of names Luiz had given him.

"The list is tentative, of course," Luiz was saying. "All the dons have responded, save for Lara and Obregon."

"See that they do. This banquet is of utmost importance. I want every landowner in California to attend."

"As you wish."

"There's something else I need you to do, Luiz. I want you to see to it that Santa Anna is informed that I've arrived in Los Angeles."

Luiz stared at him. "Santa Anna? But—"

"He's in Ensenada. Inform him that I'll contact him in a few days."

Luiz shook his head in confusion. "Why alert Santa Anna to your presence?"

Absorbed suddenly in the outcome of the contest, Montero answered distractedly. "Please, Luiz, don't question every action I ask of you."

Against all expectation, Love's opponent had edged into the lead by a nose. Montero kept his eyes on the lead rider as the horses thundered past, realizing only then that it was Elena in the saddle. "That's my daughter!" he gasped in mild outrage.

"You've raised a spirited one, Rafael," Luiz commented as they walked briskly toward the finish line. "Next thing you know she'll be plucking roosters from the sand or twisting bulls' tails like some *vaquero*. It's California's air that brings out the passion in them."

Montero aimed a furious glance over his shoulder and increased his pace. "Not in my daughter it won't."

Recapturing the lead, Harrison Love was first to cross the finish line. "Well done, señorita," he was congratulating Elena as the two dons arrived. "You almost won." Having shed his cavalry uniform for conventional shirt and trousers, Love might himself have passed for an *hidalgo*—a "son of something."

"You flatter me," Elena told him. "But in truth I barely kept up." She smiled playfully as he helped her down from the saddle.

"No, no, you ride brilliantly." Love laughed, smitten, as he looked to the ground in a bashful gesture. "Señorita, that a lady such as yourself can ride like the wind . . ." He faltered and swallowed hard.

Elena's smile broadened. "Why, thank you, Mr. Love. Or is that Captain Love? My, what a name you have. In any case, I've met few men capable of accepting a challenge from a lady—as you say—with such grace and aplomb."

Love looked flustered for a moment; then, catching sight of Montero, he turned. "Your daughter is a very impressive rider, Don Montero. Especially for a woman."

Elena bristled, and the red in Montero's face deepened. "I'm glad you found her a worthy competitor, Captain. Next time, perhaps, you'll challenge her to a wrestling match."

"Father," Elena said sharply.

He refused to look at her. "Most women of her class would know enough to ride sidesaddle in the company of men. And horse racing is hardly a proper skill for a member of the *gente de razón.*"

Love frowned. "I meant no disrespect, Don Montero."

"I hired you to run my army, Captain, not to encourage my daughter to embarrass herself in public."

Elena gave him a patronizing look—one he had long grown accustomed to. "Forgive me, Father. I would not have challenged Captain Love to a race had I known that my standing as a aristocrat would be at stake."

Montero looked at her. "You challenged him?" He cut his eyes to Love. "My apologies, Captain."

Love grunted a response. Elena smiled, took Montero by the arm, and began to lead him away. As they walked towards the hacienda, he turned to her. "You let him win, of course," Montero said conspiratorially.

Her eyes brightened. "Of course I did."

* * *

Ten paces into the mouth of the cave, Alejandro stopped and turned around to gaze incredulously at the waterfall. He then swung back to Diego, his eyes wide with astonishment.

"Come," Diego said, gesturing with his torch. "There's more."

Like Diego himself, the cave had suffered the harsh wear of twenty years of inactivity and neglect. Animals had taken up residence here; even a grizzly, judging from the scat on the floor. Tornado's stall was empty, of course, and all the oats and hay had been consumed long ago. Diego had often wondered what might have become of the stallion. He assumed that Tornado had lingered near the cave for some time awaiting Zorro's return, and had then run off to rejoin his wild brethren, perhaps in San Gabriel Canyon, where Diego had originally roped him.

Alejandro sucked in his breath as they entered the gigantic vaulted room at the rear of the cave. Even though the place was in shambles, it still retained its grandiose aura. Diego's prized swords had gone to rust and many of his prized books had been devoured by insects. Diego walked to the raised fencing area, squatted down on his haunches, and used his hand to brush aside the decades worth of dust and grime that had accumulated. Alejandro watched as arcs of inlaid concentric circles and intersecting lines began to appear. The younger Murieta, with sudden recognition, lifted the medallion to his face, comparing its design to what he now saw.

"*Madre de Dios,* it's the same!" He glanced around. "This is truly the place—the lair of the Fox." He moved around the cavern, touching things with reverent respect; then he came to the stairs. "And where do these lead?"

Diego stared at the stone stairs for a long moment before responding. "They used to lead to the parlor of the de la Vega household."

Alejandro was slow in understanding the connection, but when he did, his eyes opened wider than before. "Then you are . . ."

Diego inclined his head. "Diego de la Vega."

"But everyone thought you had died in the fire. With your wife and your child." He shook his head, as if to clear all of his swirling thoughts. "Where have you been all these years? Where is your family?"

Diego stooped to gather some of the tattered books from the floor. "I was dead," he said quietly. "We'll leave it at that."

"I remember the last time I saw you. I was just eight or so." He hefted the medallion. "The night you gave us this. You must have fought off a hundred men."

"You were just a boy," Diego said. "It seemed more impressive than it was."

"Oh, no, I do not forget. You were the greatest swordsman in all of California."

"Rafael Montero was commandant of Los Angeles then. Do you remember him?"

Alejandro's eyes narrowed somewhat. "His soldiers killed many. The night Montero left, he sentenced three men to be executed. But we knew that Zorro—we knew that you, Don Diego—would rescue them in time." He paused briefly. "I remember puppets crushed by the hooves of galloping horses. And I remember Zorro—you—placing the medallion around Joaquin's neck. You said, 'As a token of my thanks.' And you called us *'compañeros.'* " He grinned briefly. "After that night, Montero went to Spain or somewhere."

"Yes, yes," Diego said, uncomfortable with lingering too long in remembrance. "But the important thing is that Montero has returned to Alta California."

Alejandro nodded. "I've heard talk of Montero's return. He is said to be a wealthy man now, no longer a mere commandant but the *patrón* of a fine hacienda in Los Angeles. It is said that he has grand plans for California's future, and that many of the common people and the dons are taken with his ideas."

Diego scowled in recollection of Montero on the beach. "Hah! He crushed the people twenty years ago and he will crush them again!"

Alejandro stroked his shaggy beard in comprehension. "I recall another thing about Montero—that Zorro was his sworn enemy."

"As was Don Diego de la Vega," Diego said. "Therefore, he must not know that I am here."

"He knew you were El Zorro?" Alejandro asked in surprise.

"Montero had his suspicions early on. Not until the very end was he certain."

Alejandro glanced at the stairs in sudden revelation. "He was responsible for the fire. He did this to you." He waited for a response. "I'm sorry for the things I said in the tavern. You *do* know what it's like to lose family."

"It's something I don't wish to discuss, Alejandro. Nor should you ask again. Simply remember that you are to tell no one that I am alive."

"You're going to kill him," Alejandro exclaimed. "Am I right?"

Diego evaded the question. "First I'm going to learn something more about his grand designs for Alta California, and just how this Harrison Love from Texas fits into them."

"And then?"

"Then, if you're properly prepared, we will both tempt our fates."

Alejandro compressed his lips. "I should tell you one thing: I'm a wanted man." He gestured to himself. "This face is widely known along the Camino Real."

Diego appraised the beard and unruly hair. "Don't worry, we can fix it so that no one will recognize you. I know a thing or two about disguises."

Alejandro grinned widely and took up his sabre. "Then let my training begin!"

Diego circled him slowly. "Do you have the slightest notion how to employ that thing?"

Alejandro tracked him. *Cierto.* The sharp end goes in the other man."

Diego blew out his breath. "This may require more work than I thought."

Swordmaster and Pupil

"THIS IS THE TRAINING CIRCLE OF THE SPANISH School," Diego explained from the outermost concentric circle of the now fully exposed marble dais. "It was designed by the swordmasters Narvaez and Thibault." He gestured with the Toledo-steel sword given to him by the master Kendall, in Madrid. "This circle will constitute your entire world, your entire life, until I tell you otherwise. Nothing exists outside of it."

"Except Harrison Love," Alejandro remarked.

"There is nothing outside of it!" A sibilant flourish of the rapier made it emphatic. "Until I tell you so, even Harrison Love does not exist!" Diego softened his harsh tone. "Revenge, Alejandro, can be a cruel master. Vengeance heightens the senses and inspires confidence, but ultimately it clouds your judgment and betrays your attack. Do you understand me?"

Alejandro nodded.

"Do you believe me?"

"I believe you."

90

Diego nodded curtly. "Then we have made a beginning. . . ."

They had been holed up in the cave for three days, subsisting on fresh fish from the Pacific and oranges and lemons from what had once been the de la Vega orchards. Diego had eaten like the starving man he was and had gradually found his strength returning, though the decades in Talamantes and the impact of having seen Montero, Elena, and the medallion all within the space of a few days still had his mind reeling.

Clearing the cave and ordering his things had helped, and for isolated moments—cleaning the swords of surface rust, arranging the books, sweeping the floor—it seemed that only weeks rather than years had passed. Awakening from those reveries had proved difficult, however; during them, he could almost believe that Esperanza and Elena were waiting for him on the far side of the secret panel that had once opened on the house. But the reality was that the house lay in ruins, much like the charred memory of his past.

Alejandro had done most of the fishing and food-gathering, and had somehow kept himself from asking too many probing questions. Daily plunges in the ocean and the river that fed the waterfall, along with long runs along the shore had toned Alejandro's body, making him look much different from the lithe ruffian he was. All that remained of the full beard were the twin accents of a dashing, dark moustache.

Presently, Diego was patiently explaining the training circle on the dais's floor to Alejandro. "As your skill improves," Diego said, stepping toward the center of the design, "you will progress to a smaller circle. And with each new circle, you world contracts, bringing you that much closer to your adversary; that much closer to retribution."

Alejandro hung on his words. "This part I like."

Diego ignored the enthusiasm and began to walk toward Alejandro, raising his sword. "When you have completed your training—" he touched the tip of the blade to the medallion's centermost circle "—you will move to this circle, the ideal striking distance, where you will rely only on your training, intuition, and speed." He took a backward step and cut his eyes to the sword he had prepared for Alejandro. "Ready?"

Alejandro took a breath and raised his sword.

"Show me a lunge."

Alejandro complied, though awkwardly and slowly. Diego rapped the flat of his sword against his pupil's leading leg. "Your stance is too wide. Move your front foot back a bit."

Again Alejandro complied, the heel of his boot squeaking on the marble. Unsatisfied, Diego whacked his leg once more. "Turn your knee out. Out! Now, straighten up. I want a lunge, not a remise!"

He circled Alejandro while he held the pose, evaluating his posture and the set of his legs. The young man had height, strength, endurance, and speed, but he had yet to demonstrate a facility for strategy and tactics, or much in the way of focus and concentration.

"You're gazing at me as you would a horse," Alejandro said out of the side of his mouth. "Maybe you should check my teeth and gums and coat while you're at it."

"You think you're being humorous, but you're closer to the truth than you know. The alignment of your legs under your buttocks will prove to be as important as speed or accuracy. Dueling is balance, and if you fail to achieve it, you will fail at all that follows."

Diego jabbed Alejandro with his forefinger, toppling him, as if in slow motion, from his lunge pose. The sword slipped from Alejandro's grasp and clattered on the floor. Diego picked up the blade and tossed it to Alejandro as he was getting to his feet. "Balance," he repeated. "Now—lunge!"

Alejandro's movements were more determined and precise. He demonstrated more raw talent and energy than Diego recalled himself having possessed, albeit at fifteen rather than twenty-eight years. But, more importantly, Alejandro had the innate ability to dispense with thought when it suited him. Now, Diego thought, if Alejandro could rid himself of emotion as well, the true impediment to mastery . . .

"Better," Diego commented.

Alejandro glanced at the position of his feet and earned himself another whack on the leg.

"Never look at your feet. Don't even think about your feet."

"Then why are you so preoccupied with them?"

Diego disregarded the remark and concentrated on the position of Alejandro's hand on the hilt. "Don't hold it too loosely, but don't attempt to crush it either. Hold it . . . the way you might hold a woman." He fell silent for a moment, then asked, "You have held a woman, haven't you?"

Alejandro gave him a sidelong glower. "More than one."

"And yet none of them correctly, it seems." Diego sighed in frustration.

Alejandro thought about it for a moment, then resignedly altered the position of his hand.

"A vast improvement. It's clear that you're very experienced in some areas."

"You should see me with a pistol."

"I can well imagine. But anyone can kill with a ball of lead, Alejandro, and I'm not interested in turning you into a killer."

"What are you going to turn me into, then?"

"A man of honor."

Alejandro had spent the better part of the morning training vigorously. Diego had made Alejandro perform countless sets of push-ups over a tray of lit candles, while Diego nonchalantly read, resting his feet on Alejandro's straining back. While Alejandro executed intricate gymnastic routines to improve his stamina and balance, Diego would watch warily, sipping wine. Another exercise had Alejandro walking along a thin wooden beam, to either side of which hung several bags of sand tied to the timbers that helped to shore up the grotto's arched ceiling. Diego would set the bags swinging like pendulums across the beam. It was Alejandro's task to leap past each bag without touching it or the one in front of it, while somehow remaining upright on the beam. An hour into the exercise he lost track of how many times he'd been either struck by a bag or simply landed wrong on the beam and been sent sprawling to the floor.

Besides honing his physical abilities, Diego also made Alejandro change his physical appearance by sitting him down in a bathtub and cutting his long tresses back into a neat, stylish cut. Although sullen about his new look, Alejandro accepted every new task and lesson with vigor.

Just now, Diego was standing by the small shrine he had built. But rather than lighting the candles or praying, he was placing the gold cross and the ivory statue of the Virgin into a burlap sack.

"What are you planning to do with those?" Alejandro asked from the beam.

Diego didn't bother to turn around. "We need supplies, and we can't risk you being seen on the beach or foraging for fruit. I'll go to the pueblo and trade these trinkets for what we need. They mean nothing to me any longer. All that matters is your training."

Alejandro leaped defiantly from the beam. "I'm going along."

Diego immediately saw the uselessness of arguing and, resigned, simply nodded his head. "There's an oxcart going to ruin at the east end of the orchard. We'll borrow one of the mules the *ganaderas* use to haul hides to the beach."

Alejandro rubbed his hands together in expectation. "A taste of the town will do us both some good."

Two hours later they were nearing the plaza. Along the sides of the dusty road, men napped in the meager shade, knees pulled up to their chests and sombreros lowered over their faces. A few scrawny dogs hurried from the market area, with bits of unidentifiable meat dangling from their jaws. Dozens of children were about, chasing one another, flinging handfuls of dirt, making mischief however they could.

Diego had the reins of the cart and Alejandro was slumped in the back, the bag of holy objects beside him. Suddenly, three soldiers galloped past, leading five obviously unbroken horses, three mustangs among them. The sound of thundering hooves sent people scattering in all directions.

Alejandro pointed at the most ample of the soldiers. "That one's name is Lopez," he said into Diego's ear. "Aye, and look at that stallion he leads!"

Seeing the horse, Diego felt his heart race, as on the

day he had first spotted Tornado in San Gabriel Canyon. "A black Andalusian," he intoned nostalgically.

"It could be the child of your own Tornado!" replied Alejandro.

Small, swift, and hard, with a shiny jet-black coat, the Andalusian trotted proudly, even in captivity. As Diego and Alejandro watched, the horse suddenly reared back, pulling Lopez's mount up short and sending the cadet corporal himself completely out of his saddle. Freed, the stallion began to charge madly around the plaza in search of a way out, summoning both frightened and sportive shrieks from women and children, as it overturned vendors' stalls, leaped over hitching rails, and kicked up a vertible dust storm.

While his two men had their hands full trying to keep control of the mustangs, Lopez made a start after his own horse only to give sudden chase to the stallion as it neared him, and so failed to apprehend either of them.

Diego's eyes remained on the Andalusian. "He's enough like Tornado to be his ghost," he muttered.

In front of the *cabildo,* the black steed overturned a stall stocked with rebozos, serapes, and imported scarves, and was suddenly headed straight for a *patrón* and his wife, who had just stepped from their carriage. Seeing an opportunity, Alejandro was out of the oxcart and running directly into the path of the spooked horse.

"Quickly—back into your carriage!" Diego heard him tell the terrorized aristocrats while he was ushering them inside. Then Alejandro whirled to face the horse, lifting his head in an almost seraphic gesture and murmuring something indistinct that somehow confused the Andalusian into stopping in its tracks. It reared up as if to kick Alejandro with its forelegs, but instead came down on all fours, and, unbelievably, allowed Alejandro to approach and stroke its mane.

Horse thief, Diego reminded himself. *That was why he was widely known and wanted.*

Amid a storm of silk scarves blown every which way by the wind, Lopez lumbered on to the scene. Plainly humiliated, huffing and puffing like some steam engine, he angrily snatched the stallion's rope lead from Alejandro's hand. At the same time, the don had emerged tentatively from his carriage and was offering Alejandro profuse thanks for having intervened.

"I do believe you saved our lives, young man," the caballero said in a quavering voice. "I am Don Peralta, of Capistrano."

"My privilege, *patrón,*" Alejandro responded gallantly.

In a show of gratitude, the don opened his purse, prized out a *real,* and flipped it Alejandro's way. The former horse thief accepted the meager reward with theatrical graciousness.

"Why, thank you again, *exigente,*" he said with a bow.

As he was heading back across the plaza to rendezvous with Diego, a black scarf wrapped itself around his ankle and he bent to catch it before the wind whisked it away.

"That was brave but reckless," Diego remarked. "Even a wanted man who has trimmed his beard and washed the filth from his face should know better than to call attention to himself. Someone might have recognized you."

"It was worth it." Alejandro thumb-tossed the silver coin to Diego.

"Hardly," Diego told him.

Grinning, Alejandro discreetly began to pull things from his pockets and from beneath his serape: a ring, a bracelet, a letter or invitation of some sort—all of which he placed in Diego's hands.

"Maybe there are a few things *I* can teach *you,* Don Diego," he said after a moment. "I'm not certain the pupil is ready, but the master is here, all the same." Alejandro indicated the bag of religious items. "Now you can hold onto those 'worthless' objects of yours for a while longer."

Diego watched him saunter off, twisting the black scarf in his hands as he went.

A Thief in the Night

ALEJANDRO LUNGED FORWARD FROM THE PERIMETER of the outermost circle, holding his position while Diego watched from the center of the marble dais, a black bullwhip in his hand.

Without warning, the whip cracked, taking a button from Alejandro's shirt. "Again, you are too far forward!"

Adjusting his stance, Alejandro eyed his trainer. "You could simply have told me instead of ruining a perfectly good shirt. Or is this more about your practicing with the whip than my practicing with the sword?"

"Again," Diego ordered.

Alejandro withdrew his lead foot and lunged—only to feel the whip against the shirt's blousy sleeve. Beads of perspiration broke on his forehead and upper lip, conjured by mounting resentment as much as exertion. "If the shirt is not to your liking, then why not say so and be done with it," he grated.

Diego compressed his lips as he approached. "It's

your technique that displeases me, not your outfit." He cracked the whip in the air. "Now—like a man!"

Alejandro ground his teeth, then stepped back and lunged once again. When a moment passed, and his shirt suffered no further damage, he cautiously looked to Diego, who was standing with his arms folded across his chest, nodding.

"Excellent. Do the same once again."

As Alejandro prepared to repeat the move, thoughts of his dead brother streamed into his mind, off-balancing him. Even though Joaquin had always claimed, even boasted, that he would die young, Alejandro had never believed him. Moreover, his older brother was the only family he had ever really known. The padres and the neophytes at San Gabriel mission were kind to both of them, but Joaquin was the only person Alejandro had trusted.

Alejandro tried to refocus on his task, but it was difficult to suppress his memories of Joaquin. And even when he could put Joaquin from his thoughts, it would be Harrison Love who came to mind, frustrating all efforts to improve his mastery of the blade.

"Your mind is elsewhere," Diego snapped. "Again and again, I've cautioned you about *thinking.*"

Alejandro straightened from his posture and swung angrily to him. "How am I supposed to keep from thinking? Thinking is what men do. It's what separates us from the animals."

Diego planted his hands on his hips, and patiently explained. "You must let the sword do the thinking for you. You must let it master you before you can master it. You can't be filling your mind and executing your moves at the same time. One thing or the other is bound to suffer. In a duel to the death, you can't afford to have your technique suffer."

"Words, words! All you do is *talk* of dueling! The way to gain mastery is to fight!" Alejandro slashed *X*'s in the air with his blade.

Diego expelled his breath. "If you believe that, then there's nothing I can teach you."

Alejandro drew himself up to his full height. "As I told you in the *pulquería,* I never asked for your help."

Diego studied him carefully for a moment, then spun on his heels and stormed from the cavern. Alejandro fought down an urge to apologize; after all, he had only been speaking the truth. He reached into his pocket for the scarf that had come to him on the wind the previous afternoon, and he began to wipe the sweat from his face. He was waving the black silk in the air, intent on drying it, when an idea suddenly came to him.

The sun was setting by the time Alejandro reached the pueblo. Most of the vendors who displayed goods in the daily market had already closed their stalls and headed home. The plaza itself was quiet, save for in the vicinity of the fountain, where several children were frolicking.

With the black scarf masking his eyes and the rest of him sheathed in a muslin shirt and trousers borrowed, after a fashion, from Don Diego, Alejandro leaped to the ground from the roof of a low building and hurried to conceal himself among a group of horses hitched to a rail in front of the church. He bent over the watering trough there to gaze at his reflection, satisfied with the two eyeholes he'd cut in the silk, admiring the way the scarf masked his features, and how his makeshift cape, fashioned from an old blanket, flowed from his shoulders. Like a surging tide, the fantasies of his youth flooded into him.

"Buenas noches, El Zorro," he said to the image in the water. "I must say, that you look better than ever."

From the pommel of one of the saddles, Alejandro took a lasso. He was about to edge away from the horses when he spied a rider galloping straight for the rail. Certain he would be seen if he made a dash for it, he backed toward the water trough once more, his hand readied on the hilt of his sword. As the horse neared, he realized that the rider was not some drunken *vaquero* but a young woman—and a rather fetching one at that—sitting western style on a gelding. She wore a beautiful long ruffled cotton dress with a shawl but her black hair was undone and windblown, in almost daring contrast to the styles affected by the refined women of Los Angeles.

It became immediately apparent that the young woman was equally surprised to find a masked figure in black standing among the hitched horses, though her initial reaction was more one of curiosity than alarm.

"Where's the costume ball?" she asked after they had traded stares for several seconds.

Alejandro grinned and lifted his forefinger to his lips in a gesture of silence.

The woman's eyes narrowed in uncertainty. Her horse whinnied and shuffled nervously, but Alejandro caught hold of its bridle and quieted the animal, drawing an ambiguous smile from its rider.

"You should take care, señorita," he told her. "There are dangerous men about."

Her fine eyebrows arched mockingly. "Really? Should you see any, I trust you'll be sure to point them out to me."

Alejandro tipped his head to her and backed away

into the shadows. The woman watched him for a moment, then dismounted and walked toward the church's front gate.

Alejandro moved stealthily towards the side of the church, and quickly climbed to the roof. Peering down into the courtyard of the adjacent *cuartel general,* he saw only one soldier, who was leading a horse to the stable. Alejandro waited until the soldier had disappeared inside, then he leapt from the roof to the wall of the compound, and from there to the roof of the stable, whose peak ended at a wide, ceramic chimney. Draping the lasso's running noose over a finial on the peak, he began to lower himself down the chimney, twisting himself upside down as he neared the firebox of what was the stable's immense forge, so that he could peek out the opening.

The soldier he had glimpsed in the courtyard was exiting the stable by way of a grilled door that led to the *cuartel's* barracks. Alejandro let a minute pass, then righted himself and dropped to the floor. Gazing around, he spotted the black Andalusian in one of the stalls. *But first things first,* he told himself.

Through a crack where the doorjamb met the stable wall, he could see into the barracks, where some two dozen soldiers were relaxing on tiers of bunks along the one wall. Others were cleaning weapons or sharing drinks; many were seated around a table playing poker, a drunken Corporal Lopez among them.

Confident that he had the stable to himself for the time being, Alejandro gathered up a saddle and tack and moved warily toward the black stallion. Edging into the stall, he gave the horse a reassuring pat on the neck while he took stock of the beast's eyes, coat, teeth, and blink reflex.

"Ah, but you're a fine one," he whispered. "Take it

from one who has stolen many a horse in his time." The Andalusian gazed at him. "I've come to award you the great honor of carrying me—no, *Zorro,* on your back. Your name from now on will be Tornado."

Gently, he placed the short-stirruped saddle on the black's back, being careful not to cinch the straps or slip the bridle over its head until he was satisfied that the horse would tolerate it.

"We've made a very good beginning, you and me," he whispered as he led the Analusian from the stall.

Just as he was preparing to mount, however, a burst of raucous laughter issued from the barracks, along with an accusatory bellow from Lopez about being cheated. The horse grew skittish, but Alejandro managed to calm him. Planting a foot in the stirrup, he gingerly threw his leg over the saddle and sat perfectly still for a moment, holding his breath. The Andalusian, too, remained still, though plainly uncertain of Alejandro's intentions.

Alejandro patted the beast's neck. "You'll see, we will be one in spirit, Tornado." Then he nudged the horse in the sides with his bootheels, and the animal went berserk.

From the way the horse was bucking, trying desperately to unseat its uninvited rider, anyone would have thought that Alejandro had touched a red-hot branding iron to its rump. Alejandro managed to hang on, nevertheless, even after the horse kicked out two of the posts that supported the hayloft, eliciting a protesting groan from the twisting structure before it came crashing to the floor, raining hay over everything.

The barrack's door flew open on its strap hinges and Lopez and several others rushed in, only to find what had to look like a bewitched haystack leaping straight for them. Instantly they about-faced and fled back into the barracks, pulling the door closed behind them. But that hardly stopped the Andalusian. Bucking clean through the door and landing in a storm of splintered wood, the horse kicked through a full-circle turn, its powerful, lashing rear legs sending soldiers scattering for the corners of the room, the bunks, anywhere that offered a promise of protection. Front hooves flailing, the stallion reared up, finally tossing Alejandro to the floor, and went on to demolish several tiers of bunks before Alejandro was able to throw himself back into the saddle and aim the bronco for the door to the courtyard.

With a single bound, the horse repeated its door-shattering act. But this time the jump carried it so high that Alejandro's head struck the lintel of the jamb, and he was hurled to the floor once again.

Soldiers closed in on him from all sides. Alejandro rolled, crawled, and somersaulted to avoid their clutching hands and stomping feet. The urgent acrobatics carried him into a weapons room, where a cannon had been eased back from a *tronera*—a firing hole—perhaps in preparation for a cleaning. Except for the firing hole, however, the room's only exit was the very doorway Alejandro had rolled through, which was now congested with soldiers, jockeying to be the first to have a go at him.

With nothing to lose for trying, Alejandro scrambled to his feet, grabbed a torch from a wall sconce, and touched it to the fuse at the cannon's breech.

He was dumbfounded when the weapon discharged, all but deafening him and leveling almost the entire front wall of the building. Coughing from the dust and sulfurous stench, the soldiers, flattened to the ground with their arms over their heads, looked up to see Alejandro laughing uproariously, as much in relief as in incredulity at what he had inadvertently accomplished.

Tossing the torch aside, he put his fists on his hips and struck a heroic pose. "Let it be known far and wide, the legend has returned!"

Those soldiers who had lifted their heads were now gazing in terror—not at him, however, but off to his left where the torch had landed in a trail of gunpowder spilled from a keg overturned during Alejandro's rambunctious entry. Comprehending that he wouldn't be able to make it over the razed wall in time, Alejandro raced the sputtering flame to the keg and picked it up to carry it out the door, trampling several soldiers as he did. But, realizing too late that the keg was continuing to leak powder in his wake, he saw that the flame was now catching up with him!

With a panicked yell, he heaved the keg back into the weapons room and fled for the *cuartel's* door, rushing through just as a powerful explosion launched hellish fire and pieces of flaming wood high into the darkening sky.

The explosion blew Alejandro from his tenuous hold on the wall onto the grounds of the church. When he had recovered enough to recognize where he was, he made a mad dash for the church's side entrance. It was almost time for vespers, but the only person in evidence was Father Felipe, striding past a candle-studded shrine to San Sebastian toward the confessionals at the rear of the building. Confronted by a masked figure in head-to-toe black, the padre stopped short and frantically crossed himself twice in rapid succession.

"Dios mio, Santa Maria," he uttered. "Is this some vision or have you actually returned?"

106

Alejandro stared at him. "Returned?"

The Franciscan took a cautious step forward. "But how can it be you, Zorro? It's either true that you are supernatural, or the years have been much kinder to you than to me. . . ."

Alejandro cleared his throat meaningfully. "Padre, quickly," he said. "I need sanctuary."

Father Felipe grew almost giddy. "Of course you do, of course you do, Zorro." He clamped his hands on Alejandro's shoulders. "And believe me, my son, we need you now more than ever—"

"But unfortunately I've no time to talk of those matters, good father. You must hide me."

From outside came the sounds of footfalls and soldiers barking orders. The priest hurried to the door, closing and barring it. He was beaming when he turned around. "Why, it's just like the old days!"

Alejandro was already hastening for the only hiding place within sight: a tall, cloth-roofed confessional booth with two ornately carved doors. Slipping into the priest's side, he lowered himself to the wooden bench, catching his breath.

"Father, are you all right?" a female voice asked from the far side of the partition.

Alejandro froze.

"Father?"

He shrunk back into the cramped space. Outside, soldiers were pounding on the church door. When the woman rapped on the partition, he had no choice but to slide open the door that concealed a window of tightly woven wooden latticework.

"Uh, have no concerns, my . . . child. Everything is fine."

"Father, what's going on? It sounds like a battle is in progress outside the church."

"Have no fear." Alejandro cleared his throat. If he could play Zorro, why not a friar as well? He lowered his voice to add, "You are safe in the house of the Lord."

"Telling words, Father."

"You think so?" Alejandro asked despite himself. "I am very new at this."

"New at this? But how could you be, Father Felipe?"

"Father . . . no, no, my child. You see, I am Father Juan—visiting from the Santa Barbara mission." He bit his lip in concern when the woman fell silent for a long moment. Then he saw her cross herself.

"Forgive me, Father, for I have sinned. It has been three days since my last confession."

"Three days?" Alejandro interrupted in surprise. "How many sins could you have possibly committed in three days? Why, even the territory's most wretched desperados scarcely have time for one serious sin per week. Perhaps you should consider returning when you've had more time to err."

Again, the woman fell silent for what seemed an eternity. "Pardon me, Father, but I'm not sure I understand."

Alejandro risked leaning toward the partition in an attempt to identify just who was doing the talking. When he did, he saw the large and lovely eyes of the young woman he had encountered at the hitching rail.

"Just a small joke, señorita, uh, my child," he said. "Proceed with your confession."

"Father Juan, I fear that I may have broken the Fourth Commandment."

"Ah, you stole something, yes?" Alejandro said confidently.

108

"What has theft to do with the fourth commandment, Father?"

Alejandro winced. "I was merely testing you, child. Please, be more specific."

"I dishonored my father."

"That's all? Well, maybe your father deserved dishonor. Maybe he's a *cabrón?*"

The woman leaned forward as if to peer into Alejandro's space. "Father Juan," she said in a firm voice, "exactly what kind of friar are you?"

"What kind? Well, we at the Santa Barbara mission take a slightly different approach to confession. Does the notion of change frighten you?"

"Not at all. In fact, I welcome change."

"Then, please, continue."

She took a breath. "You see, it's just that I try to behave properly—the way my father wishes me to. But I sometimes worry that my heart is too wild for that of the daughter of a caballero."

Alejandro arched an eyebrow. "A caballero, you say. Which caballero would that be?"

"You don't need to know that, do you, Father?"

"No, I suppose not . . . But tell me more about this wild heart of yours."

"I also—" She faltered.

"Yes?" he said, too eagerly.

"I've had impure thoughts regarding a certain man."

"Recently?"

"Just today. Actually, only moments ago."

"Santa Maria."

"And I fear he might be a bandit."

"Really? Black mask, husky voice, ruggedly handsome?"

109

"Yes. And when he looked at me . . . Well, I mean, when I looked at him . . . Father, I felt as if I was *on fire*. I felt—"

"Heat in improper places?" Alejandro prompted her. "The sound of the ocean rushing in your ears? The blood pounding in your veins?"

"Yes, and more."

"You felt lustful?"

The woman lowered her head. "Yes."

Alejandro smiled, impressed with himself. "We have a slightly new policy regarding lust as well. A more lenient policy."

"Really?" the woman said, almost coquettishly. Then she remembered herself. "Just a moment. A more lenient policy? Who are you?"

Sudden commotion in the church told Alejandro that the soldiers had gained entrance. "This is a house of God!" Father Felipe told them in loud protest.

It was the voice of Harrison Love who answered him. " 'To subvert a man in his cause, the Lord approveth not.' Lamentations three, thirty-six."

"Leave my church!" the Franciscan said. "You have no—"

Love cut him off. "Search everywhere: the chapel, the loft, even the sacristy—he has to be somewhere." To Father Felipe he added, "I will deal with you later, Padre."

Alejandro glanced overhead at the confessional's fabric roof, then leaned toward the partition a final time. "Señorita, you've done nothing to warrant a penance," he whispered. "Trust your heart—it won't lead you astray. Now—go. In peace." He closed the small door and waited for her to leave. As he was about to do the same, he heard Love speak to her from the other side of the confessional.

"Señorita Montero, what are you doing here? Are you all right?"

"Montero!" Alejandro whispered to himself.

"I was merely confessing, Captain Love. The question is, what are *you* doing here?"

Love ignored the demand. "Confessing to whom, señorita, when Father Felipe is right here?"

"Why, to Father Juan. From the Santa Barbara mission."

"Stand aside, if you please, señorita," Love exclaimed after a moment. "You've been duped. There's a dangerous desperado on the loose."

Alejandro didn't waste a moment. He was already scampering through the fabric ceiling and out into the loft when a hail of lead tore the confessional to pieces.

The Fox Lives!

ALEJANDRO MADE HIS WAY ACROSS THE CHURCH loft and out onto the roof without any of the soldiers seeing him. Bellying to the edge of the roof, he looked out over the *cuartel,* where small fires were still loose in the outbuilding near the barracks. Those soldiers that weren't formed up in bucket brigades were searching the grounds for the intruder. Not too far away from the opposite slope of the roof stood the black Andalusian, munching contentedly at scrub grass.

"Tornado!" Alejandro whispered elatedly. *"Psst!* Come here, boy."

The stallion ignored him.

"Get over here—*prontissimo!*" Alejandro warned, "or Zorro will be riding someone other than you."

Impatient, he risked a quiet whistle, which succeeded in getting the horse's attention—at least to the effect that he glanced up at the roof and walked the few feet it took to position himself directly below Alejandro.

Smugly confident, Alejandro jumped feet first, and might well have landed in the saddle had the black not taken two additional forward steps. Instead, he hit the ground hard and promptly fell on his rear, which merely inspired the horse to give him a look of seeming disinterest. Determined now, Alejandro leaped to his feet and vaulted over the horse's rump into the saddle.

"This time I'm on your back for keeps!" he announced. Laughing triumphantly, he heeled Tornado into motion and galloped through the confusion surrounding the *cuartel,* pausing only long enough to carve a Z with his blade into the building's adobe wall.

Whip in hand, Diego paced back and forth across the mystical symbol devised by the Spanish School, trying to imagine where his short-tempered pupil might have gone. Surely he hadn't given up so soon, though Diego wouldn't have blamed him if he had. The retribution Alejandro sought against Harrison Love wasn't complicated by old rivalries and the future happiness of the only person in the world who mattered. No, the horse thief Murieta could simply procure himself an *escopeta* or a pistol and be done with it. Love's life for Joaquin's, cut and dried. But Diego wouldn't be able to do as much to Montero until Elena learned the truth about her past and was at least willing to accept Diego into her life.

Glancing at the dais's innermost circle, it struck him that that space was as much Montero's as his own; notwithstanding the cruel turn of events, Montero had become Elena's father, and Diego was powerless to alter the events of twenty years earlier, or all that had happened since.

He uncoiled the whip and was moving it about aimlessly when he heard movement at the mouth of the cave. Turning, he was stunned to see Alejandro, costumed in his makeshift Zorro garb, mounted on the black stallion that had wreaked havoc on the plaza some days earlier. Judging by the look on Murieta's face as he dismounted, he seemed to be expecting applause.

"Well, what do you think?" he asked finally, adopting a rakish pose.

Diego stared at him, expressionlessly; then he flicked the whip at a nearby lighted candle, extinguishing the flame.

Alejandro beamed. "I not only stole the horse, I left a Z on the wall of the *cuartel*. By morning, everyone in Los Angeles will be whispering your name once again."

Diego's whip extinguished two more candles.

Alejandro swallowed and found his voice. "The people will be speaking the name of Zorro, again, Don Diego!"

"What they say is of no consequence," Diego said at last. "All they will see is a fool. You steal a horse and scribble on a wall, and you think you've earned the right to wear that mask?"

Alejandro looked abashed. "But I was as agile as the original Fox. You should have seen—"

Diego flicked the whip straight at Alejandro, tearing the mask from his face and ripping it in two.

Alejandro's body tensed. "Careful, old man," he warned.

"Zorro was not some circus buffoon, some seeker of applause or fame! He was a *servant* of the people. He did whatever was needed to improve their lot."

"And now he is needed again—"

114

The whip cracked again, tearing away Alejandro's cloak. Even so, he held Diego's furious gaze. "I didn't ask for your help in the cantina. But I came here to learn how to fight like you, to have your strength, your courage. Now, when I try to use what you've taught me, you slap me down." He risked a forward step. "I'm tired of all your training, your endless lecturing. Tired of waiting for you to tell me I'm ready. I have my own scores to settle, a new life to find. I thought I could begin here, but I guess I was wrong."

Diego stared at him, wondering about the son he might have had had Esperanza lived. But resolve and ardor and emulation weren't enough. "I won't give my blessing to a man who looks as though he has been out playing in the dirt. You shall have it when you earn it and not before." He threw the whip aside and drew his sword. "Draw your blade."

Alejandro took a backward step and showed his weapon. Eyes locked, they began to circle one another before engaging blades. Ignoring what Diego had taught him, Alejandro began to slash wildly at Diego's sword, determined to use his greater strength to push Diego back toward the rear of the cave. Diego parried each powerful strike, but Alejandro was undaunted and continued to press the attack, arcing his blade left, right, and overhead. His face was mottled with anger and he expelled his breath through gritted teeth as he lunged forward. Diego fixed his gaze on Alejandro's eyes, then, without betraying so much as a hint of his intentions, he sidestepped the charge and extended his foot. Flailing his arms for balance, Alejandro stumbled forward, managing to remain on his feet. But by the time he had righted himself and whirled around, the tip of Diego's sword was poised against his throat.

"Lesson number one, Alejandro: Never attack in anger." Diego withdrew his blade. "You'll have my blessing when you earn it, and not a moment before," Diego repeated solemnly.

Montero and Love meandered through the smoldering shambles of the *cuartel,* while soldiers continued to salvage what objects they could and exercise the horses. The sun had only been up for a little over an hour but the air was already balmy.

"The priest—Felipe—aided in his escape," Love was saying. "But as of today he'll be ministering to a whole new flock of lost lambs, if you take my meaning."

Montero nodded. "Duly noted." His eyes roamed over the wreckage. "How could one lone intruder cause so much destruction?"

"Well, he had the help of a bronco for part of it—a black Andalusian Lopez and the others captured a few days back."

"Where is this horse now?"

"The thief made off with him. From the way he handled himself, I'd say he's no stranger to the game."

"Some *vaquero* turned desperado, then?"

Love shrugged. "Hard to say—what with the mask and all."

Montero came to an abrupt halt. "Mask?"

"Black bandanna. Wore it over his eyes and head." Love demonstrated, then motioned Montero over to the wall. "Here's something else I thought you'd be interested in seeing before we got rid of it."

Montero gaped at the zigzag mark that had been slashed into the wall's stucco surfacing.

Love tilted his head to one side. "Maybe it's only a tipped-over *N.*"

Montero flashed him a look. "Save your retorts for someone who appreciates them, Captain. You know as well as I do what this mark means."

Love shrugged. "To me it means that some bandit is hoping to stir up trouble by masquerading as an old legend. We both know it can't be the same man who rode roughshod over this pueblo twenty years ago."

Montero appraised the Yankee for a long moment. "Explain yourself, Captain. How is it that we *both* know?"

Love didn't quite smile. "I'm only saying, Don Montero, that the *hombre* who broke into the *cuartel* last night was a young man. The real Zorro would have to be . . . practically your age."

Montero reached out and touched the Z, running his fingers along the rough edges of the wounded stucco. When he withdrew it, his hand was trembling slightly. "Find the one who did this and see to it that he is hung in the plaza."

Nearby, a group of soldiers stopped their work to stare uncertainly at Montero, who unconsciously rubbed his neck where his personal trio of slashes was concealed by the high collar of his brocaded jacket. "And have this *letter* removed from the wall immediately."

Diego cracked the whip, prompting Alejandro to advance, then retreat along a radius line of the design. To enforce the precision of his stance, a length of cord bound Alejandro's feet together. Upon reaching the circumference of the penultimate concentric circle, Alejandro turned and executed a fleché—advancing by leaping off his leading foot. And upon encountering the next of the bisecting lines, he turned and executed a balestra—a forward hop, followed by a lunge.

117

Nodding in approval, Diego coiled the whip in his hands. "You may yet reach the point where people will think of you as a swordsman."

Alejandro glanced at him. "You had years to perfect and hone your skill. I've had days."

"Stop making excuses for yourself."

"I'm not. What I say is fact."

"What you say is irrelevant." Diego motioned to the rack of swords on the wall. "Choose your weapon."

Alejandro compressed his lips and moved the rack. Unsheathing an epee, he waved it about, slashing the air.

Diego watched him for a moment. Then, as if by magic, he displayed a silver soup spoon in one hand, and a sheet of parchment in the other. Eyebrows knitted in curiosity, Alejandro lowered his blade.

"This was among the things you pilfered from the don in the plaza. It's an invitation to a banquet Montero is hosting for caballeros from throughout the territory." Diego flourished the parchment. "But I suspect that this is more than some *tertulia* or fandango. I think it figures into his designs for Alta California. And it will be your pleasure, Alejandro, to attend—as a spy."

Alejandro gave his head a rapid shake. "If I can't pass for Zorro, what makes you think I could pass for a nobleman?"

"Because I plan to endow you with something that is even further from your reach than mastery of the sword—charm." He rose to his full height and lifted his chin, as if posing for a portrait. "Charm, Alejandro, is the key to the world of Montero and his kind. Breeding, social skills, refinement—they are the true

118

possessions of the *gente de razón*. In Montero's case, those and his daughter."

"Ah, now she is *true* beauty."

Diego's head snapped around. "How do you know that?"

"I met her," Alejandro explained affably. "When I was hiding out in the church confessional."

Diego averted his gaze. "She is the finest creation of God's hand."

Alejandro tilted his head. "You would like to have her, Don Diego?"

Diego flushed with rage. "You could think such a thing of me, scoundrel? I appreciate her beauty as I would—" he searched for an apt comparison "—a painting by Goya or Velazquez."

Alejandro knew enough not to press the point. "I apologize. I mistook your meaning."

Regaining composure, Diego allowed a nod. "We must convince Montero and the rest that you are a gentleman of stature, perhaps recently arrived from Spain—"

"But I don't know Spain, Don Diego."

"All right, Mexico, then. You do know Mexico, don't you?"

Alejandro smiled. "All the way south to Oaxaca."

"Then we'll work with that. If we can succeed in convincing Montero that you're entirely guileless—"

"Guileless?"

"Harmless. A mere dandy—"

Alejandro's eyes widened with misgiving. "I have to play a dandy?"

"Try to think beyond yourself for a moment," Diego said firmly. "If Montero views you as even the slightest threat to his enterprise, he will keep you

119

outside it. If, on the other hand, he feels he has nothing to fear by your participation—or that you might even contribute some celebrity to it—he may just invite you into his circle." His eyes stayed on Alejandro. "Then we will know for certain what he plans for the people of California."

Reluctantly, Alejandro reached for the soup spoon and turned it about in his hand, as if it were something strange and baffling.

Diego watched him and shook his head. "This, too, could take a good deal of work."

Montero's Fandango

SANCHO TO ALEJANDRO'S QUIXOTE, DIEGO climbed
from his donkey to lend his *patrón* a hand in dismounting. Made to look other than the wild Andalusian he
was by way of an ornate saddle and tack that had once
belonged to his namesake, Tornado allowed himself to
be led away by one of Montero's grooms.

The lion-fountained yard fronting Montero's opu-
lent hacienda was filled with a score of equally fine
horses, along with fancy carriages and *coches,* some of
which had come from as far away as Branchiforte and
Yerba Buena, and still wore the dust of the Camino
Real. The men—*empresarios, ganaderos,* and *cor-
regidores*—were dressed in pressed, ruffled shirts, stiff
cummerbunds, waist-length formal jackets, and silk-
lined hats with gilt bands. Emerging from the padded
comfort of their coaches, the women displayed themselves in decorative short-sleeved gowns of silk or
calico, kid shoes, colorful waist sashes, and intricate
necklaces of gold and silver. Some wore high combs
in their long hair.

121

It occurred to Diego that the wealth and power of all of Alta California was represented—the governor-general himself was said to be there—and he couldn't help but be reminded of yesteryear at the de la Vega household—or of the dreams he had laid out for Esperanza on their final night together.

Decked out in some of Diego's ageless caballero finery—velvet pantaloons, a red waist sash, and a rich blue velvet jacket—Alejandro appeared to blend well with the crowd, unless one realized that his eyes were open a trifle too wide and that his dashingly mustached upper lip was beaded with perspiration.

Concealing his utterances behind a silk handkerchief, he said to Diego, "This is definitely the most foolish thing I've ever done."

"I doubt that," Diego answered, more to himself.

"We'll never get away with it."

"We will." Diego brushed the dust from his pupil's jacket and leaned close to him. "A nobleman is nothing more than a man who says one thing while thinking another." He made his voice haughty. "'What a pleasure it will be to see you,' the aristocrat says. When he's thinking: 'In a coffin.'"

Alejandro nodded uncertainly. "But what about you? What if Montero recognizes you?"

Diego loosed a short laugh. "He won't, because he would never chance being caught looking a servant in the eye."

Alejandro exhaled. "I've a sudden sense of . . ."

"Excitement?"

Alejandro shook his head. "Impending doom."

Diego adjusted the fit of his pupil's jacket. "Good luck. And, most of all, remember not to let the dons out of your sight."

They moved together toward the hacienda's massive round-topped front doors, where a servant glanced at Alejandro's filched and altered invitation and announced him to those gathered in the foyer.

"Don Alejandro del Castillo y Garcia."

Montero himself turned at the announcement and watched Alejandro as he entered and approached, dipping on one leg and inclining his head in greeting.

"Why, I haven't encountered that in years," Montero said in pleasant surprise. "The formal greeting of the Spanish court." Surrounded by some of Los Angeles's *hacendados* and *rancheros,* he was sporting short breeches and white stockings, a rich waistcoat, and leather shoes imported from Massachusetts.

Alejandro gave Diego a sidelong glance before replying, "My father was very strict about matters of etiquette."

Montero lifted an eyebrow. "And who exactly *is* your father, young man?"

"Was, your Excellency. Bartolo del Castillo."

Montero's other eyebrow went up. "I knew of Don Bartolo, of course, though I never had the pleasure of meeting him."

With studied arrogance, Alejandro extended his hand to Diego, who placed in it a land grant document he drew from the pocket of his own jacket. "My servant, Bernardo," Alejandro said by way of rote introduction. "In any event, Don Montero, I have just arrived from Mexico City—by way of Mazatlan and Ensenada—to inspect our family holdings in the north, and it was suggested that I call on you."

"And why is that?"

"Well, you see, my mother is quite close to Queen

123

Isabel. And Her Royal Highness, who is something of an historian, spoke highly of your former work here."

"Really?" Montero said in obvious wonder. "I would have thought that my recent dealings with President Santa Anna would have put me out of favor with the Spanish Crown."

"Not at all, I assure you. Mexico, after all, is still the scion of Spain. And I'm informed that Alta California in particular remains a land of opportunity—for men of vision."

Montero stroked his bearded chin. "And you view yourself as a man of vision, Don Alejandro?"

"Let us say, a man in search of vision."

Montero smiled and nodded.

"But I must apologize for intruding," Alejandro said quickly. "Perhaps I could call again when I won't be interrupting a gala."

"Think nothing of it. I would be honored if you would join us."

Alejandro inclined his head. "The honor is mine, señor."

Montero gestured Elena forward. "May I present my daughter, Elena. Elena, Don Alejandro del Castillo y Garcia."

Alejandro gazed into her eyes and lowered his lips to her hand. "Charmed. Though I find myself without a gift for the hostess—ah, wait a moment." Catching even Diego off guard, he executed a simple trick Joaquin had taught him years earlier, and conjured a rose out of nowhere. "In want of a full bouquet, a single flower must suffice. For you, fair señorita."

Elena accepted it with intrigued amusement and thanked him.

Aware of Montero's appraising look, Alejandro nodded curtly and continued on to the inner courtyard. "Come, Bernardo," he said imperiously over his shoulder. "And pick up your feet."

Well before eight in the evening, Montero's gala was already underway. Servants bearing trays of food and drink maneuvered among candlelit tables, while an orchestra comprised of violins, guitars, trombones, and trumpets played festively. At the back of the paved courtyard, on a raised platform, well-heeled couples danced with old-fashioned formality. Pedestals garlanded with fragrant floral arrangements lined the yard, scenting the air.

Seated among wealthy dons and dueñas from Santa Ines, San Luis Rey, and San Carlos, Alejandro called for more drink. "Bernardo, fetch me more champagne!" To his tablemates, he added, "A good champagne needs to have a certain icy fire in its veins, don't you agree?"

Diego stiffened but complied. Too many glasses of Montero's snow-chilled imported champagne had loosened Alejandro's tongue and made him more the fool than the dandy he was supposed to be. Diego was encouraged that his pupil had managed to come as far as he had, but he quietly chastised him as he refilled his glass with the bubbly wine.

"You're overplaying your part. 'A certain icy fire in its veins,'" he echoed in derision. "Rein in your performance before you fall off the stage. And observe the angle of your wrist, if you expect to succeed."

Alejandro leaned back foppishly in his chair. "I must say that I prefer you as a servant. Yes, servitude brings out your better qualities." His words slurred together.

Simmering, Diego was about to respond, when both he and Alejandro saw Elena approaching. Diego moved away, risking the briefest glance at Elena.

"Don Alejandro," she said. "My father and I would like you to join us at our table."

Alejandro stood, teetering slightly but managing nonetheless to take her arm. "Nothing would delight me more, señorita."

Diego watched them leave; then, picking up a tray of wine glasses, he made his way out of the courtyard and into the east wing of the hacienda.

At the host's table, much to Montero's own disquiet, polite conversation had turned without warning to the subject of the recent "assault" on the *cuartel* and the familiar mark rumored to have been carved into the wall.

"Believe me," Don Hector was saying, "Zorro is the least of our concerns—even if he is the same man who terrorized this territory twenty years ago. Why, I'm willing to wager that he's too old to sit in the saddle for more than an hour at a stretch."

Montero grimaced. "If, as you say, he is the same man, he would be my age exactly."

Hector fumbled for words. "But, uh, desperados are said to age faster than men of wealth and standing."

Montero forced a laugh and clapped his peer on the back, encouraging the other dons to laugh along with them. In fact, Montero had already investigated the possibility that Don Diego had somehow returned to Los Angeles. The warden at Talamantes had sent word that, while the prison's guards had successfully repressed a riot, a guard had been killed and one man was, in fact, missing. There was no record of the prisoner's name, though the other inmates had referred to him as El Silencioso—the Silent One.

Hector's mollifying remark about desperados was being repeated around the table as Elena and the young dandy from Castille arrived. Montero stood and introduced him to each of the members of his inner circle. "And this is Captain Harrison Love," he finished. "If not a caballero, a man of kindred spirit."

Alejandro proffered the Texan a limp hand. "Captain Love," he mused. "Are you not the same Harrison Love who is said to have recently engaged a bandit of some legendary reputation?"

Love's craggy face took on color. "I'm still in pursuit of him. Although he's hardly 'legendary,' Don Alejandro."

Alejandro adopted an expression of mock surprise. "Is that so? Well, with any luck at all, it won't require as much shot to bring him down as it did the church confessional."

Restrained laughter escaped the dons, and Montero as well, who watched Love's embarrassment turn to jealousy as Alejandro held a chair for Elena.

"Besides, no one knows for sure if it's the same man," Love blurted. "Anyone can knot a silk bandanna around his head and pretend to be the Fox. A mask, at least, never grows old."

"Which only complicates the problem," Alejandro returned. "For a mask can't be killed."

Montero nodded sullenly. "Well stated, Don Alejandro. Well stated."

* * *

Diego threaded his way through Montero's rambling *casa mayor,* past brass urns, potted plants, a piano, gilded statues from Guadalajara, and oaken furniture from the United States. What with his servant's garb and tray of glasses, no one paid Diego any mind, and he was ultimately able to pass beyond the hectic atmosphere surrounding the courtyard and into the residential wing. He wasn't looking for anything in particular; merely something he could use to expose Montero's scheme, which in his heart he knew to be nefarious.

Turning a corner into a broad hallway softened by plush Persian carpets, he found himself confronted by a sturdy, uniformed guard holding an old flintlock. That someone should be posted so far from the festivities guaranteed the significance of the closed room at the man's back.

Holding the tray aloft, Diego continued along the corridor without hesitation. In passing, he noticed an open room just opposite the guard, and yet he continued to move on without being questioned, slipping at last into another open room just beyond the first. Hastening to a doorway that opened on the adjoining room, Diego set the tray down and quietly cracked the door. As he had surmised, he could now see through the open corridor doorway to the guard.

With no time to waste on subtlety, Diego snatched a glass from the tray and threw it to the floor. The guard's ears pricked up and he hurried into the room, seemingly without concern that someone might be lying in wait for him.

Stepping from the shadows near the fireplace, Diego brought a iron poker down on the guard's head as he was bent over examining the shattered glass, knocking him unconscious. Relieving him of a ring of keys, Diego recalled his escape from Talamantes, and he thanked God for his continuing good fortune.

Quickly and quietly, then, he crossed the corridor to the closed door and let himself in.

Rivals

IN MOUNTING PANIC, ALEJANDRO STUDIED HIS PLACE
setting—a bewildering array of cutlery that included
half-a-dozen spoons, almost as many forks, and a
couple of oddly shaped knives whose specific purpose
he could scarcely imagine. Already he had mistaken a
fingerbowl for a soup bowl. Fortunately, most of the
dons had been too engaged in separate conversations
to notice his error, and Elena was speaking privately
to Love.

Alejandro was studying Montero for cutlery clues
when he saw him whisper something into the ear of
Don Luiz. Luiz then accepted a key from Montero
and left the table. Worriedly, Alejandro glanced
around for Diego. Feeling Montero's eyes on him, he
made himself the picture of nonchalance.

"Captain Love is a most interesting man, Don
Montero," Alejandro began, while servants set down
plates of beef, pork, venison, and *paella*. "Wherever
did you find him?"

"We originally met in Madrid, where the captain

was a mercenary for Spain in its war against the French in Morocco. Then we met again in Mexico City, after the captain had fought for Texas independence at the side of Samuel Houston. Once more, I was impressed with him as a soldier and a leader. When California becomes independent, he will command our army."

"Independent?" Alejandro said. "I've heard nothing of this?"

Montero affected a little sniff. "Nor are you likely to—outside this room. But, yes, my goal is to see this territory become a sovereign republic."

"With Captain Love as its general," Alejandro said more harshly than he had planned. "Is he not of somewhat . . . humble origins for a young woman of such obvious distinction?"

"Meaning what, Don Alejandro?"

"Well, only that he and your daughter appear to be smitten with each other. I would have thought—"

"Captain Love may be smitten, but Elena is quite another matter. I assure you, she will marry appropriately."

"To, say, a Spaniard of noble lineage?"

Montero's eyes narrowed somewhat. "It's merely a matter of finding the right person." He paused. "Do you know of such a man?"

"I dare say there must be one at this gala," Alejandro told him with elaborate casualness.

In what was obviously Montero's private study—a richly appointed room with a vaulted ceiling—Diego stared in anguished disbelief at a portrait of Esperanza that hung on the wall behind Montero's desk. From her apparent age, it had to have been executed during the years Diego had spent in Spain. When he could endure no more of the memories summoned by the painting, he turned away from it to survey the rest of the room. The only other object that drew his interest was a locked, iron-banded traveling chest that sat against the outside wall.

Moving to it, he tugged at the lock, then stopped when he heard footsteps in the corridor. By the time the imposing oak door opened, Diego had concealed himself behind a large armchair. Montero's chief supporter, Don Luiz, entered, and moved directly to the chest. Unlocking it, he lifted the lid and rummaged through the chest's contents until he had retrieved a small, lacquered box. He then relocked the chest and departed.

Diego lingered for several seconds, then followed.

"Who exactly is this Zorro person?" Alejandro put to the table. "When I first heard the name, I assumed that everyone was discussing fox-hunting—of which I have never approved. All those noisy dogs."

"An anarchist who fancied himself a Robin Hood," Don Hector answered. "A bandit so cunning he fooled the very people who looked upon him as their protector. Now, what with Santa Anna's neglect, the peons imagine Zorro's return in every amateurish act of vandalism."

Elena turned to her father. "But why would the people so embrace him if he was nothing more than a bandit? Some of the townspeople—even our own servants—seem almost jubilant at the prospect of his return."

"I'll dismiss them immediately," Montero snapped, though the remark drew unintended laughter from the dons.

Love looked from Montero to Elena. "He's no protector of the people, señorita. Most of the stories you hear about him are closer to fairy tales. Just what you might expect from uneducated laborers and Indians."

The governor-general, a stout man with a flowing beard, cleared his throat meaningfully. "It has always been my belief that those who govern must hold themselves above the people they rule—so as to determine what's best for them, of course."

"Of course," Elena replied, with obvious sarcasm. "But until the people are free to govern themselves, I suspect we'll find Zs carved into many a wall." Abruptly, she turned to Alejandro. "What is your opinion, Don Alejandro?"

Determined to enact the role Diego had created for him, Alejandro patted his mouth with a napkin. "I agree with the governor: sheep require a shepherd— and certainly not a bandit leader. Zorro's mask and sombrero probably conceal a bald head and unsightly features."

The jibe elicited amused laughter from the dons. Elena, however, was not willing to settle for facile remarks. "I'm sure there are some who consider him heroic."

Alejandro made a gesture of dismissal. "Heroism is but a romantic illusion."

"Much like nobility?"

"Elena!" Montero reprimanded sharply.

"Heroism doesn't necessarily have to be righteous," Love said, coming to Montero's defense.

Alejandro sniffed. "Spoken like a true soldier. All that sweaty swordplay, gunplay, horseplay . . . It's enough to give any gentleman a frightful headache."

Elena scowled at him. "And just what is the proper work of a gentleman—climbing in and out of carriages?"

Alejandro sighed with purpose. "No, my dear. Proper work would be increasing one's holdings—so as to ensconce young ladies such as yourself in lavish comfort."

Elena turned away in disgust, while Montero favored Alejandro with an agreeable smile.

"Unfortunately, our quality of life is threatened by lawlessness," Alejandro went on. "I myself have been *this* close to several notorious bandits. And let me assure you, unless they are made to fear our collective strength, anarchy will prevail."

Elena exhaled wearily. "I'm sure they have much to fear from you, Don Alejandro."

"But he speaks the truth," one of the dons commented. "Why only the other day, in the plaza, a purse-snatch robbed me."

Alejandro squinted at the man, recognizing him only then for the caballero he had saved from Tornado's wild run through the streets. "Shocking," he said quickly, feigning outrage. "What kind of animal would stoop to such an act?"

Elena pressed her lips together. "One who is hungry, perhaps."

Alejandro made a fatigued sound. "I couldn't really comment on hunger. But then again, señorita, neither could you."

Montero laughed while Elena burned. "A woman's grasp of politics," he said to Alejandro. "What more can I say?"

Love broke the uneasy silence that descended over the table. "Hey, this is a party, isn't it?" He pushed

back his chair, stood, and bowed stiffly at Elena.
"May I have the honor of this dance?"

Out of a sense of propriety, Elena glanced at her
father for permission. At his nod, she accepted Love's
hand and moved with him to the dance floor.

Elena decided that she had nothing to lose by
flirting with Love. He was coarse and somewhat
brutal, but he was obviously attracted to her and she
couldn't deny his skill, albeit with guns and horses.
Not that her father would ever approve a liaison. But
better Love than a dandy like Don Alejandro, with his
scented handkerchief and supercilious confidence. If
only he wasn't so pleasant to look at she might be able
to dismiss him out of hand. But those dark eyes and
the grace of that body. . . . Then, too, there was
Zorro—or at least the man who had stepped into the
part. When he wasn't pretending to be a friar, that
was.

She still blushed when she recalled their hushed
exchange in the confessional, of all places. But what
were the chances of encountering him again? And just
what sort of man lurked behind that silk bandanna?
Some buckaroo or *vaquero?* The servants claimed that
the original Zorro had been a disaffected nobleman,
but was that true of his successor as well?

Her eyes strayed over the courtyard as Love escorted her to the dancing area. Could one of the men
her father had gathered be a traitor to the cause? And,
really, what cause was that? As near as anyone could
tell, the Zorro who had slipped into the *cuartel* had
come to steal a horse!

Unless the horse had been his to begin with? It was
all too confusing.

The orchestra was playing a waltz.

Love led gamely, if inadequately. He was as stiff on the dance floor as he was in conversing with her. But she didn't let that throw her off. She had danced in the arms of dozens of men—in Spain, Mexico, Argentina—and she knew how to make herself appealing, with a smile, a glance, a bare arm draped over the shoulder of her partner—

Suddenly, she noticed Don Alejandro standing behind Love, staring at her with candid interest. All her careful technique was abashed. She turned red.

"Have you nothing better to do than stare?" she asked sharply.

Love whirled, startled and irritated to see Alejandro—a rival, at least in his eyes. "You looking for something?" Love demanded.

Alejandro shrugged. "A miracle in everyday life."

Love squared his shoulders. "Yeah, well, go look for it somewhere else. Elena and I are trying to dance."

"You are trying, Captain. Only she is succeeding." Instantly, Alejandro smiled apologetically and bowed his head to Love. "Forgive me for giving voice to a tasteless joke at your expense—though I hope it won't be the last." Before Love could even respond, he added, "Don Montero wishes to speak with you."

Love blinked stupidly, bowed to Elena, and reluctantly moved off, leaving Elena and Alejandro eyeing each other. After a moment, he opened his arms in a graceful gesture of invitation and she accepted.

Diego returned from his brief reconnaissance in time to see the conclusion of Alejandro and Elena's flowing, almost sensuous waltz. Conflicting emotions tugged at him, but he scarcely had time to sort through them when he saw Montero and the dons rising from their table and preparing to move into the house. Their somber faces and hushed conversations made it clear that an important meeting was about to take place, and here was Don Alejandro the spy, out on the dance floor.

Diego stood where he could catch Alejandro's eye as the dancers' polite applause was waning. With a covert nod, he indicated the departing dons, his expression conveying a sense of urgency.

Alejandro responded quickly—though not in the way Diego might have imagined—by calling to the leader of the orchestra.

"An *jarabe tapatio* if you please."

Dancers returning to their tables stopped and the musicians grinned with enthusiasm. The piece they commenced was called "El Sombrero Blanco", a lively tune that was said to be all the rage in Mexico City.

Alejandro had turned to Elena. "Do you feel equal to the task of attempting something more robust?"

She tilted her head, then smiled sweetly. "My only concern is for your distaste of perspiration, Don Alejandro. But if you are equal to the task, I most certainly am."

She set herself in an almost defiant posture as the dance began. Hands tightened on the lapels of his short jacket, Alejandro moved around her like a flamenco dancer, his boot heels tapping accents on the paving stones. All at once the pompous caballero was a strutting bantam cock, and the transformation roused her. As their movements became bolder and bolder, other couples withdrew on all sides to allot them more floor space for their wild turns and twists. It was a dance of seduction and counterseduction, of advances and rejections; a mating ritual. Elena was not like some fandango peasant with eyes cast to the floor and feet immobile under her long gown; she held Alejandro's gaze as he circled her, at once coquettish and brazen. People clapped in time to the beat, and cheered the dancers as they would the moves of a matador.

Montero and the dons had stopped to see what the commotion was about. Harrison Love wore a look of bridled vexation, and Montero was livid. As he stormed toward the orchestra, Diego heard him mutter, "This girl is simply too willful. Wild like her mother."

The remark pierced Diego's heart, and for a moment he wasn't even aware that the music had come to an abrupt halt. Alejandro had stepped away from Elena, who was nonchalantly patting her hair back into place, like some lover caught at a midnight rendezvous.

Alejandro saw Montero hastening toward him and immediately fell back into character, altering his posture from one of sportive self-confidence to stuffy propriety.

"Well, if that's the way they're dancing in Mexico City these days, I'll take Madrid," he said loud enough for Montero and Diego to hear.

Puzzled by his sudden change in attitude, Elena swung to confront him, but by then Montero was upon them.

"Don Montero, excuse me," Alejandro said, pretending surprise, "I must take a moment to catch my breath. Your daughter is a very spirited dancer."

Montero shifted his glare from Alejandro to Elena. "Spirited? You are to be complimented for putting it so delicately."

Elena's eyes flashed in angry disbelief. Shoving Alejandro aside, she hurried from the dance floor, just as Diego was moving within earshot of Montero and Alejandro.

Montero watched her for a moment before saying, "I apologize if she offended you."

Alejandro patted his forehead. "Completely unnecessary. She is young and impulsive, but her beauty is incomparable, and she has the commanding presence of her father. It would be my great pleasure to introduce her at court."

Montero inclined his head. "Elena and I would be honored."

"Between the two of us," Alejandro said conspiratorially, "we could make her the toast of Madrid, Mexico City, or wherever you choose to introduce her formally to society."

Montero clasped Alejandro's shoulder. "Speaking of introductions, young man, if you would care to join us in my private courtyard, there is something I wish to share with you."

Intrigued, Alejandro said, "Why, whatever might that be, Don Montero?"

"A vision of the future."

The Treachery Revealed

*A*T CONSIDERABLE EXPENSE, MONTERO HAD HAD HIS round table engraved with the fighting bull and bear he envisioned as symbolic of the embryonic nation of California. Watched over by a shade tree, the table sat in Montero's torchlit private courtyard, and just now at its center rested the lacquered box Don Luiz had retrieved from Montero's study.

Some members of the inner circle were already seated; others, including Alejandro, were standing. Montero had positioned himself by a long curtain, which promised surprises.

"Fellow caballeros of Alta California," he was saying, "two decades ago, Spain acquiesced to the demands of a group of mestizos and granted independence to Mexico. All of us, however, have fond memories of the golden years when we ruled this territory in the name of the Crown, determining its destiny." His voice grew heavy with conviction. "My friends, the time has come to reclaim what was ours. I give you: the Republic of California."

The curtain dropped away at the pull of a cord, unveiling a canvas map of North America that depicted the new republic, stretching south from the frontier with Baja California clear to the Oregon Territory, and from the Pacific east to the Rocky Mountains. Many of the dons greeted the map with polite if ambivalent applause; a few of them actually frowned.

"Look at the precarious situation we face as Californios," Montero continued. "Each day sees the arrival of more Boston men and foreign mariners, of new pronouncements by the *alcalde* of Los Angeles against the *alcalde* of San Diego, or of escalating rivalries between Monterey and what is already being called San Francisco. To the south, we have a nation led by a one-footed general who wars with France over damages to a French restaurant; and to the east we are pressed by the ever-expanding United States, with its proclamations of Manifest Destiny."

"Are you proposing revolution?" Don Aguilar of Branchiforte asked. "If so, think hard of what happened in Texas. Santa Anna promised autonomy and instead rode north with the black flag of no quarter."

"Perhaps Don Montero fancies himself another Sam Houston," Don Cota of San Jose suggested.

Montero waved his hand. "Our secession is to be a bloodless one. Revolution and massacres are unnecessary, because we are going to *buy* our independence."

Don Peralta—whose belongings Alejandro had lifted—stood up from his place and began to pace around the table. "Don Montero, every man here owes you something for what you did to turn our former riches into absolute wealth. Of course, you made certain to take a healthy percentage of all that you accrued, but business is business. Now, after

141

twenty years, you return to a territory we have been governing—largely in lieu of any guidance from Santa Anna—and your first act on debarking from the vessel that brought you here was to accuse us of being thieves."

Some of the dons grumbled assent, but Montero was unfazed. "Come now, Don Peralta, I was merely playing to the expectations of the peons. Certainly you would done the same—"

"And what are you doing now if not playing to the peons?" Peralta asked with surprising intensity. "You speak of 'buying' California from Santa Anna. I, for one, find it difficult to believe that El Presidente would part with California for any amount. Not only is he soured by what happened in Texas and New Mexico, it was at his urging that California be extended to the 42nd parallel."

Montero nodded. "I grant you that. But at the moment Mexico is heavily in debt to both England and Spain, and Santa Anna's coffers are empty. Even this so-called Pastry War cost him six hundred thousand pesos. More to the point, Don Peralta, he has *already* accepted my offer. In fact, even as I speak he is on his way to Los Angeles to seal the deal."

The dons traded glances of incredulity and concern. "And with what do you intend to pay him?" Don Peralta asked. "You must be aware that whatever terms were discussed surely surpass what we could raise, even by pooling all our resources." He paused to allow his words to sink in. "You're nursing a dream."

Montero merely smiled. "Very well. But let us all live the dream together." He moved to the table, opened the lacquered box, and held up for everyone's inspection a bar of pure gold, prominently stamped with the Spanish imperial seal.

"Tomorrow, we will take a trip into the mountains, where I will lay all your doubts to rest."

All but Luiz recognized the remark as their cue to depart. As the other dons were filing from the courtyard, he lingered a moment by the canvas map.

"You should have told me, Rafael," Luiz said when Montero approached.

"A general tells his lieutenants only as much as they need to know."

Luiz turned to him. "But I thought we had a business arrangement. You gave me the land, I mined the gold. Now you tell me that I must forfeit my profits to help you realize a dream."

"We are noblemen," Montero replied in a scornful tone, "not merchants. Money was never my goal. It was always my vision that we should rule this territory—as we were destined to."

Luiz shook his head. "Destiny, again. As *you* were destined to, Rafael. My goal was merely to be rich."

Montero's nostrils flared. "Do you honestly think that I would return after all these years to fulfill a 'business arrangement'? I thought you knew me better than that." His expression softened and he clapped Luiz on the back. "I haven't forgotten your loyalty, my friend. When I rule California, you shall be at my side."

Luiz forced a smile. "You're too generous."

The meeting over, Alejandro was searching for Diego when he all but bumped into Elena in the hacienda's central courtyard, where the gala, too, was winding down.

"Leaving so soon, Don Alejandro?" she said, pretending concern. "If only I hadn't promised Captain

Love that I would wait for him, I would gladly usher you out—oh, excuse me—*to* the door."

Alejandro smiled tightly and inclined his head. "Charming, to the last. But you needn't bother yourself on my account. You see, your father has already invited me to spend the night."

Elena's jaw fell. "What—here?"

"Well, of course here." Alejandro issued a short laugh.

"In that case, I certainly hope you'll find your quarters to your liking," she said in a grudging tone.

Alejandro sighed. "I'm sure they'll suffice." He glanced around the courtyard. "After all, it's not as if Los Angeles were Mexico City."

Her eyes narrowed. "It was my understanding that you preferred Madrid—where the dancing is more *genteel.*"

Alejandro blinked. "Ah, you're referring to the comment I made to your father. But couldn't you tell that I was only jesting?" He shook his head. "I keep forgetting what life is like in the provinces. But perhaps you'd allow me to make amends. What would you say to a serenade below your balcony?"

Elena was momentarily confused. "Do you sing, Don Alejandro?"

"Me? Of course not. But I could send my servant Bernardo to sing and play for you."

Elena's eyes flashed with anger. "By all means. I'll send my servant to the balcony. She's very fond of music."

"And where, pray tell, will you be?"

"As far from you as this house permits."

Alejandro gestured dismissively. "Do what you must—if you don't trust yourself being close to me."

Her eyes widened. "Trus—It's *you* who are not to

144

be trusted, Don Alejandro. One moment you're the courteous caballero; the next, you're . . ."

"Yes?"

Elena swallowed. "Let's simply say that you're quite the chameleon."

Alejandro showed her a roguish grin. "I know the benefit of a good disguise, if that's what you mean, señorita."

She stared at him for a moment. "What are you saying?"

He shrugged. "Only that we are often forced by circumstance to act out certain roles. You, for example, are very adept at playing the mannerly young woman, when I suspect that you're more comfortable in riding clothes than in silk gowns."

Elena averted her gaze. "I can't imagine why you'd think that."

"No? Then I will tell you: I see it in your eyes. You are different than your father."

She looked up at him. "He would not be pleased to hear you talking like this, sir."

Alejandro smiled. "Need he hear of it?"

"Would you not have me confide in him, then?"

"No, of course not. But one thing: I hope that I, too, may someday be worthy of your confidence."

Elena almost smiled. "Good night, Don Alejandro."

He dipped his head. "And to you, señorita."

"This trip had better be worth it," Don Peralta was remarking, early the next morning. "My backside feels like that of a whipped mule."

"That is quite fascinating," Don Julio rejoined, having grown impatient with the old man's constant complaints. "Because I noticed just the other day in the vapor baths that your backside actually *resembles* that of a whipped mule."

Scowling, Peralta ignored the laughter and rapped his knuckles against the canvas that covered the coach's window. "Montero doesn't even trust us."

"Would you?" Don Hector asked, to another chorus of laughter.

Driven by soldiers from the Los Angeles garrison and led by Montero and Love, on horseback, the convoy of coaches had departed the hacienda at sunrise. But now, after a jostling four-hour ride over rugged terrain, Alejandro sensed that they were finally reaching their destination. And despite the coach's black canvas wrappings, he had a rough idea of where they were.

As the coach came to a halt, Alejandro completed his silent calculations. They had traveled in a northeasterly direction from Los Angeles, perhaps not far from the foothills near the San Fernando mission. Still, he doubted that he would be able to retrace the route for Diego, who had remained at the hacienda with the other servants.

The coach doors were opened by one of the soldiers, and Alejandro and the bone-weary dons climbed out into sunshine so bright that it briefly blinded them to the very sight Montero had brought them so far to see. Nearby, other dons were stepping down from similarly shuttered coaches, uttering like complaints about the glare. When their eyes adjusted, however, they found themselves looking into a narrow canyon, where a mining operation was in full swing all around them.

A flutter wheel had scooped most of the water from a narrow river, whose bed was ravaged by holes and nearly picked clean of stones. Wooden flumes, timber scaffolding, ladders, and platforms climbed above the riverbed, providing access to mines that had been excavated from the canyon walls. Crisscrossing the terrain were narrow gauge tracks outfitted with handcars filled with rubble and tailings.

Alejandro grasped that the mystery of the territory's "disappeared ones" had been answered; for the whole of the operation, from sluices to mineshafts, was being worked by captives in shackles and chains—many of them Indians, woman and child alike—under the command of armed men. Swallowing his fury, he surveyed the scene. His attention was drawn to one of the few clothed figures amid the slaves; he saw that it was Father Felipe.

"Welcome, gentleman, to El Dorado," Montero announced.

"Gold," Alejandro said in a daze. "You've discovered *gold.*"

"Actually, an Indian did," Montero said. "While searching for some stray horses, he found a gold nugget among some wild onions. I was one of the first to receive word of the find, and this—" he gestured broadly to the canyon "—is the result."

Montero and Love led their astonished guests to a crude stairway that switchbacked down into the canyon. Along the way they passed several natives crushing stone to slurry, which was being hauled away by others to an *arrastra,* of the sort that had long been in use in Mexico.

A primitive form of smelter, the *arrastra* consisted of a circular, shallow, slurry-filled pit that had been gouged out of bedrock and was lined with closely fitted flat stones. A heavy boulder, suspended from a wooden crossbeam by a length of chain was dragged around the vat by horses, but more often by slaves, who were cheaper to replace. Into the vat flowed a steam of diverted water, which carried the lighter sand out through a discharge hole, leaving behind the heavier particles of metal.

"At first, we were literally picking placer gold from the river," Montero was explaining. "But now that we've discovered the mother lode, we're involved in digging and smelting."

"But these workers," Don Aguilar sputtered, "where did you find them?"

"Anywhere we wanted." Montero snorted. "All of them are law-breakers who have been sentenced to hard labor."

Alejandro watched with distress a young boy staggering under the weight of a load of slurry. Exhausted, the boy paused for a moment, only to be severely kicked back into motion by one of the guards. It took a moment for Alejandro to realize that he had seen the boy before—at the water station where he, Joaquin, and Three-Fingered Jack had relieved Cadet Corporal Lopez of a rat-infested strongbox.

"So this is the future of California," Alejandro said, careful to keep the revulsion from his voice.

Montero puffed out his chest. "Exactly." Noting a general lack of enthusiasm among the dons, he added, "Gentleman, you surprise me. Recall, if you will, the adage among the Yankees who come here to settle and are forced to abandon their Protestant faith: 'A man must leave his conscience at Cape Horn.' Is there one among you who is not guilty of exploiting the peons?

"For twenty years, Don Luiz and I have kept this operation going, without breathing a word to any but our most trusted agents. And believe me when I say that secrecy has not been easy. I suspect, in fact, that all of Alta California is rich with gold. But should the rest of the world learn of what has been discovered here, we would be quickly overrun, and our dream for independence would be finished."

Just then, an explosion rocked the area, resonating in the canyon and raising a huge cloud of dust and debris.

"Calm down, everyone," Love said. "The blasting is just part of the mining process."

Montero continued his guided tour, ultimately leading the dons deep into one of the mines, where a small room had been hewn out of solid rock. One end of the room was partitioned by thick iron bars, behind which were burnished stacks of gold bullion. Savoring the dons' obvious awe, Montero unlocked the door to the enclosure.

"By rights, of course, all you see belongs to Santa Anna, but fortunately for us he is unaware of its existence." He picked up one of the ingots. "I've had all the bars marked with the Spanish seal, to convince Santa Anna that the gold has come from the crown." He set the bar down. "Now do you understand? Within a week's time we're going to buy California from Santa Anna with gold dug from his own land!"

Returned to the glare, Montero was leading everyone to the smelter room when a wild scream came from one of the men operating the handcars. Squinting, Alejandro recognized the whooping worker as none other than Three-Fingered Jack himself—though near starved and plainly loco.

"Welcome to hell's outhouse, caballeros!" he screamed, brandishing a miner's pick at the transfixed dons. "They may call us the disappeared ones, but take a look around. As you can see, we haven't disappeared—we've simply been *relocated.*"

Love stepped forward, using his hand to shade his eyes. "I know you, *hombre.*"

Jack grinned madly. "Of course you do. You shot me in the leg and had me brought here. I'm the illustrious Three-Fingered Jack. And you—all of you—you're nothing but murdering bastards in fine clothes."

"Ignore him," Love said, sneering. "He's a common thief."

"Thief?" Jack yelled back. "Thief, yes; common, never. Though nothing compared to you *gentleman.* Nothing. I stole *plata,* horses, food. You, you filthy devils, you steal *lives.*"

Jack released the handbrake with a swift kick, and the car came hurtling down the narrow tracks, straight down the slope toward Alejandro and the others. Jack was still swinging the ax overhead as the dons scattered and Harrison Love calmly stepped to one side, raised his rifle, and shot Jack through the chest.

Jack sailed out of the car and hit the ground with a dust-raising thud. Silence fell over the dons, and the entire quarter of the mining operation, as the body bounced, rolled, and finally came to rest facedown in the dirt, not a meter from Alejandro. Instinctively, he knelt down beside Jack's body and gently raised his head. Their eyes met as Alejandro used his handkerchief to blot a trickle of blood at the corner of Jack's mouth. Three-Fingered Jack's crooked smile confirmed his recognition of Alejandro. But before he could muster the strength to say anything, he died.

Love was studying Alejandro as he got to his feet, his face a mask of repressed emotions. On the ground lay the partner Alejandro had run with for four years, the man who had saved his life in Mazatlan and again in San Diego, the friend who was almost like a brother to him. Alejandro ground his teeth together as Love sauntered over to Jack and used the tip of his boot to turn him faceup. Gazing down at Jack, the Texan laughed disdainfully.

Alejandro's gaze turned polar. "Something amusing, Captain?"

"More strange than amusing," Love told him nodding. "You see, this is the second time I've shot this man while he was flying through the air."

"Must be your passion for skeetshooting," Montero said before Alejandro could respond. He then turned to the dons. "Naturally, we can't tolerate insubordination or escape attempts. Secrecy is paramount."

No sooner had Montero moved off toward the coaches than the guards began to impose renewed order, employing whips, gun butts, fists, and feet, whether needed or not. Trailing the other dons, Alejandro cast a backward glance to see Love squatting alongside Jack, his bowie knife to the dead man's left wrist. An image of Joaquin rushed uninvited into his thoughts, but he forced himself to continue climbing the slope, as if nothing untoward had occurred. Just short of the coach, however, Love intercepted him.

"You and I need to talk," the Texan said from the saddle of his horse. "Back at the *cuartel*. Just the two of us."

Alejandro acted preoccupied. "Not today, Captain. Perhaps some other time."

"Today," Love corrected him. "Just the two of us." He reined the horse around and trotted off to join Montero.

Out of the Past

$\mathcal{A}$WAITING THE RETURN OF THEIR *PATRÓNES* TO
Montero's hacienda, many of the servants busied
themselves cleaning carriages or tending the horses.
Diego had led Tornado to the stable and was so
absorbed in grooming the horse, so lost in reveries of
his former life, that he had begun to sing softly
himself, and thus failed to notice Elena standing
nearby, watching him.

"Good afternoon, Bernardo," she said. "I'm sorry I
interrupted your song. Your voice is very soothing."

Diego quickly averted his eyes. "It was for the
horse, señorita. Don Alejandro's horse is very high-
spirited, and high-spirited creatures need to hear
soothing songs."

"I see."

Diego turned away from her and began to comb
Tornado more firmly.

"How long have you served Don Alejandro, Bernardo?"

Diego snorted. "It sometimes seems interminable."

Elena's laugh made him aware of his gaffe. "Forgive me, señorita. I speak out of place."

"Don't worry, Don Alejandro won't hear of your words from me." She paused for a moment. "He's a puzzling man, your *patrón*. One moment he seems as prissy as a silk stocking; the next he behaves like some *vaquero*. The way he dances, the way he looks at me . . . It's as if he's two completely different men."

She picked up a brush and began to work alongside Diego. The care she demonstrated made him think of Esperanza, and the memories made him think he might pass out from sheer heartache. Almost before he realized it, he said, "You so resemble your mother."

Elena turned to him. "My mother? But how could you possibly know that?"

"I mean that you look nothing like Don Montero, so your beauty must obviously come from your mother."

Elena laughed again and returned her attention to Tornado's shiny coat. "I don't know about that. But I do know that my father wishes I behaved more like my mother did. She was apparently very obedient to him. And always appropriate."

Diego bit down on his lip, then asked, "Is that how he describes her?"

"Yes. Although I must admit that I have my doubts."

Diego hid a slight smile. "Why is that? Because you feel that she must have been more like you?"

Elena sighed. "Perhaps it's just that I want that to be so. It would be a way of knowing her." She grew reflective. "When I was young, I used to sneak out of my room at night and ride my horse through the hills of Andalusia. My *ninera* once told me that the departed can see people in the moonlight; so I used to

153

wave at the sky, in the hope that my mother would recognize me."

Diego gazed at her. "You must have been quite a sight." He returned Elena's smile, then added, "What became of your mother?"

"She died giving birth to me. Father rarely speaks of her. He finds it much too painful."

"I know what it's like to lose a loved one," Diego said softly. "A daughter, long ago. When I see you, I remember what it felt like to be a father. I'm sure your mother would have been very proud of you."

"Why, thank you, Bernardo." Elena studied him for a long moment, as if forming a question she was afraid to ask. "Bernardo, I have to ask . . . Have we ever met before?"

"Why do you ask, señorita?"

"I'm not sure. Something about your voice, I think, or the song you were singing. I'm almost certain I've heard it somewhere."

Diego struggled to control his emotions. "You may have heard it, señorita, though how could you have heard it from my lips, since I haven't been to Spain since before you were born?"

Elena considered it, then shrugged. "Well, yours is a very pleasant voice, nonetheless."

"I'm glad that you think so."

Elena put the brush down. "Good day, Bernardo."

"Good day . . . Elena." She had started to leave when he called to her. "Your mother must have been a wonderful woman." He watched her move off, then leaned his forehead against Tornado in tormented misgiving.

The coaches didn't return until late afternoon. Alejandro had spent most of the trip in internal

154

debate as to whether to agree to Love's demands that they talk. His indecision owed less to any fear that Love would unmask him as a counterfeit don than to a conviction that he would kill Love the moment the two of them were alone—now for Three-Fingered Jack as well as for Joaquin.

By the time the convoy reached the Los Angeles pueblo, however, Diego's countless lessons had cooled his blood. Alejandro had come to accept that Love's death, while slaking his own thirst for revenge, would only incite Montero's wrath. He and Diego would be forced to flee for their lives before they had a chance to expose the former commandant for the slavemaster that he was. There was also Elena to think about. What if she were to learn that he was really Alejandro the desperado rather than Don Alejandro the wealthy Castillian? Though an unexpected development, his undeniable attraction to her figured almost as strongly in his decision as his desire to measure up to Don Diego's faith in him.

Alejandro had no sooner stepped down from the carriage than Love beckoned him to follow him to his office in the *cuartel*. The two of them sat down opposite one another at the captain's desk, a pitcher of wine between them. The noise of work crews repairing the barracks filtered into the room.

"Do you know that there are savages in Brazil who cannibalize their slain enemies in order to absorb their power?" Love was asking. He had taken a glass from the deck, but was filling it with something that was concealed from Alejandro's view—mescal or *aguardiente,* perhaps. "The eyes, in particular, are sought after. The ability to see through the eyes of an enemy is the most desirable advantage."

Love brought the glass to his lips, sipping at some

brownish concoction and regarding Alejandro with malevolent suspicion. "It's in a man's eyes that you find the true measure of his soul, don't you think?" Again, he sipped from the glass, then bowed in sudden, if feigned, courtesy. "But where are my manners, Don Alejandro? Would you care for a drink?"

Alejandro expected him to pour from the ceramic pitcher, but instead he produced the lidless container from which he had apparently filled his own glass and slid it across the desk, giving it a spin with his fingers.

The pickled head of Joaquin rotated into view.

Alejandro's entire body tensed, at once suppressing shock, nausea, and unbridled rage. In order not to betray himself, he tried desperately to keep a cool, controlled countenance.

"A different vintage, perhaps?" Watching him intently, Love shoved the pitcher forward, so that Alejandro couldn't help but see the three-fingered hand it contained.

"From the man you killed at the mine, I take it," Alejandro managed to say in a level tone.

Love snorted. "Good guess."

Alejandro sniffed and cleared his throat. "I must say, Captain, that you are a very sick man."

Love pretended to make light of the remark. "Heads in water jars, hands in wine pitchers. Yeah, I suppose it must strike someone of your . . . breeding as odd."

Alejandro played back to him. "Well, for one thing, I think you should dismiss your housekeeper." He nodded to Joaquin's head. "Tell me, who was this unfortunate one?"

Love leaned forward. "Last night at Don Montero's table you asked me about my pursuit of legendary bandits. Well, here's one I caught. His name was

156

Joaquin Murieta, and he has a brother who is soon going to meet the same fate. In fact, his name is also Alejandro. Tall man with a thick mane of black hair and a wild beard. But I don't suppose you've seen anyone who answers to that look?"

"On the contrary, Captain, I've seen many who answer to that look." He picked up a little silver cup from the table. After dipping it into the jar, Alejandro raised it to his lips and said, "To your health and good fortune in finding him." Suppressing his nausea and wrath, he made himself sip from it, as Love had.

Love nodded, almost in a show of respect. "A Murieta or not, you're less than you pretend to be, bucko."

"Or more," Alejandro said rising from the chair and patting his lips with the handkerchief spotted with Jack's blood. "And maybe someday I'll get to see what I look like through your eyes."

He marched from the office, aiming himself toward the *cuartel*'s front gate. Once outside, he angled around to the side of the building, refusing to give thought to anything until he was alone. Then, in an attempt to put to rest a small amount of his murderous rage, he snapped his caballero's cane violently across his knee.

Elena had made a habit of wandering about the daily market in the plaza, where Yang Na Indians from San Gabriel and Chumash from Santa Barbara sold fruit, vegetables, colorful woven goods, and fanciful wooden carvings. While hitching her horse to a post, she had noticed an aged native woman watching her, and now the woman was following her as she passed by stall after stall of trade goods. Then, all at once, the woman was alongside her, pressing a yellow shawl—a *pañuelo*—into her hands.

Elena stopped and smiled at the tiny figure beside her. "It's lovely," she remarked.

The woman said something in her native tongue, then touched Elena's shoulder, urging her to wrap herself in the shawl. Delighted, Elena did so, admiring the tightness of the weave and the feel of the soft wool. When she went to offer her compliments, however, Elena realized that the woman had hurried off into one of the nearby stalls, ostensibly to speak with a young native girl.

Elena approached and waited for them to acknowledge her. When they did, she directed herself to the girl. "What value does she place on the shawl? What is the cost?"

The girl translated for the old woman, who merely shook her head. "She says that it is a gift," the girl explained. "In honor of your mother."

Again, Elena told herself.

"She says that she loved your mother very much," the girl continued.

Elena frowned in confusion. "Please tell her that she must be mistaken. My mother died long ago—in Spain."

Long before the translation was complete, the old woman was making dismissive gestures. With impassioned insistence, she indicated Elena's face.

"She says that there is no mistaking the daughter of Diego and Esperanza de la Vega." The girl listened to the woman for a moment. "She says that she was your nursemaid. She hung flowers on your crib when you were but an infant."

Elena returned the shawl with a trembling hand. "Please tell her that I cannot accept her gift."

The old woman shook her head in refusal and disappeared into the rear of the stall. "It belongs to you now," the girl said. "You must keep it."

On the ride to the cave, Alejandro had told Diego of his experiences at the mine, and of his more recent encounter with Harrison Love. Diego had tried to convince him that he had acted prudently in both episodes, and that he was proud of him; but Alejandro's rage and frustration were not so easily calmed. Like a caged animal, he paced ceaselessly across the dais, muttering about what he would do to Love at the next opportunity. Diego finally had to resort to setting himself in Alejandro's path to get him to listen to reason.

"Do you think you could retrace the route to the mine?"

Alejandro shook his head distractedly. "Montero made sure we couldn't see."

"Then you must enter Montero's house tonight and take whatever papers you can carry from the chest in his study. Search for a map. We need to learn everything we can of his correspondence with Santa Anna and the terms they have agreed on. Nothing else matters."

"That jar matters," Alejandro snapped at him. "I'll see that jar for the rest of my days—"

"Your brother was dead long before you saw it. You must try to put him from your mind until we have exposed Montero's barbarism and treachery." Diego paused, then softened his tone to add, "We often lose the ones we love, Alejandro, and even revenge can't alter that." He placed his hand on his pupil's shoulder and pointed to the floor. They were standing in the

159

innermost of the dais's concentric circles. "You are ready. It is time for Zorro to return."

The grief in Alejandro's eyes was evident. "Perhaps I was once ready, but no longer. People are dying every day at Montero's mine and all I can think about is killing Love."

"And you will have your chance to do that soon enough," Diego assured him. "He will come into your circle, Alejandro. There is no need to chase him."

Alejandro took a deep breath. "You told me that Zorro was a servant of the people. So how do I keep their best interests in mind when my heart overflows with hatred?"

Diego proffered the mask of Zorro—not the black silk scarf holed by Alejandro's knife and torn by Diego's whip, but the original mask Diego had fashioned more than twenty years earlier. "With this." He raised the mask and tied it around Alejandro's head, in a gesture of investiture. "Hide your grief and hatred behind this."

"Thank you," Alejandro said soberly. "For your confidence in me."

Diego gave his shoulder a paternal squeeze. "You've earned it. Now, we must ride quickly to Montero's home. You will scale the wall at my signal."

"What is the signal?"

"You will know it when the time comes."

The remains of the de la Vega household stood on a bluff overlooking the ocean. Fire-charred adobe walls rose from the brambles and coarse grasses that had overtaken the place in the twenty years since the fire that had allegedly claimed the lives of the three members of the family. According to the account given by the mestizo who had agreed to guide Elena to the ruins, Diego, Esperanza, and a small infant, whose name had either been Esmeralda or Elena, were the victims of the blaze.

The mestizo had refused to come any closer to the place than the trail that continued on to the beach. Elena's own sense of apprehension had almost kept her from approaching, but her curiosity had finally gotten the better of her, and now she was inside the walls, effectively moving from room to room, picking her way through weeds and scrub.

The shawl the Indian woman had given her was around her shoulders, and the woman's words were loud in her ears. But accepting, for the moment, that she was actually the daughter of the de la Vegas meant accepting that her father had had some reason to lie to her about Elena's mother having died during child-birth. Twenty years earlier, he had been commandant of Los Angeles pueblo. Was it possible that he had had a liaison with Esperanza de la Vega? And yet even that flew in the face of the Indian woman's words, that the child she had obviously mistaken Elena for was the daughter of Esperanza and *Diego* de la Vega. Unless, of course, Diego had been unaware of the affair his wife had had with Rafael Montero. . . .

After some prompting, the mestizo guide had also revealed that some believed the de la Vega child hadn't died in the fire; rather, that she had been taken from California.

Elena meandered through the ruins, hoping to stumble upon some clue to the mystery, but the blackened walls and woodwork and rickety staircase told her nothing. Pausing at what had obviously been a window that looked out on the rolling water, however, a familiar smell came to her on the offshore breeze, and she realized at once that its origin was a tall, flowering bush directly under the window. The flowers were identical to those in the bouquet she had been given on the beach.

Romania, someone had said.

Tormented by doubt, a sudden weakness overtook her and she slumped down on the broken remains of a wall and buried her face in her hands. She wrapped her arms around her knees and inhaled the fragrance, recalling—for no reason she could establish—the melodious voice of Don Alejandro's servant, Bernardo.

Zorro Strikes!

LEANING BACK FROM THE ROUND TABLE IN THE MONteros' private courtyard, Love and Luiz puffed contentedly at cigars while the don himself could barely sit still. Blanketing the table were documents and letters Montero had removed from the lockbox in the study, among them a map of the canyon mining operation.

"Santa Anna has agreed to meet with us tomorrow at noon," Luiz was saying. "Ten miles east of Los Angeles—and we're to supply the gold then."

Montero looked at Love. "Well?"

Love glanced at the map and nodded. "The bullion will be stamped and ready. I don't see a problem."

"Send word to Santa Anna," Montero told Luiz. "Tell him that we agree to the terms. At noon tomorrow he shall have his gold."

Luiz stood up, drained his brandy glass, and left the courtyard. Montero waited until Luiz was gone, then added, "And I shall have California." He lifted his brandy snifter to Love in a toast to their success, grinning smugly.

The Texan returned the toast. He had barely opened his mouth to reply when cries of "Fire! Fire!" issued from the vicinity of the kitchen. With Montero hot on his heels, Love raced into the house. The broad hallway didn't smell of smoke, and when they burst through the kitchen doors, they found nothing more than the usual staff, seeing to their ovens and pots. But when the cries reached them once more, Love and Montero hurried to the nearest window and threw open the shutters, hoping to locate the source of danger.

On a grassy hillside, in plain view, the zigzagging flames of an enormous Z lit up the night.

Perched on top of the hacienda's perimeter wall, Alejandro—in the flowing silk and satin of Zorro— watched a squad of mounted soldiers gallop toward the fires Diego had set on the hillside. When the soldiers were some distance off, he leaped to a balcony in the east wing and edged through an unlocked French door into the dark room beyond. He was moving toward a doorway at the far end of the room when he happened to glance out a window that overlooked Montero's private courtyard. Illuminated by torchlight, the bull and bear round table was littered with papers, prominent among them a map of the Los Angeles basin and the surrounding territory.

Alejandro retraced his steps to the balcony and scrambled down into the courtyard. He was already angling for the table when he heard footsteps and spied Montero entering the courtyard from the other side of the arcade. Without hesitation, Alejandro launched himself straight up, grabbing hold of the top of a pillar that supported an overhanging veranda, and hauled himself up as Montero hastened for the table.

Too preoccupied to lift his gaze, Montero quickly began to gather the documents while Alejandro hung by his fingertips only two meters above him. In seeking to adjust his grip, however, Alejandro inadvertently backhanded a potted plant, which teetered and dropped from the edge of the veranda. Reflexively, Alejandro shifted to a one-hand grip and, with his free hand, just managed to snag the plant before it fell to the ground. Almost immediately, though, the slender roots began to give, threatening to send the pot plummeting.

Montero paused in his task, perhaps sensing that something was amiss, and cast wary glances around the courtyard—everywhere but overhead. His fears allayed, he scooped up the last of the documents, including the map, and hurried back inside the house.

No sooner had the don disappeared from sight than the weight of the ceramic proved too much for the plant's meager root system, and the pot fell, shattering on the cobblestones. Alejandro followed it down a moment later and moved out after Montero, silent as a shadow.

Stealing down a dimly lit and unoccupied hallway, he chanced upon the study Diego had described. The door was ajar, but the vaulted room was empty. Hung on the wall behind the desk was a large portrait of a woman Alejandro initially took to be Elena, but on closer inspection appeared to be Elena's mother, apparently painted when she was not even twenty years old. He was still marveling at the similarities when voices alerted him to the presence of two men in the hallway. Desperate for concealment, he looked left, then right, then—recalling his narrow escape in the courtyard—overhead, where a ceiling cross beam loomed just within reach.

With a leap, he grasped the edge of the handhewn timber and threw his feet over the top, so that he ended up facedown on the beam, his legs supported on an adjacent one. Not seconds later, Love and Montero entered.

"Did you dispatch men to the hills?" Montero was asking in obvious agitation.

"They're on the way," Love assured him.

"Then double the guard on the wall."

"I'll see to it." They crossed the room to the desk, and Montero set the map and the documents down. Love added, "But, remember, we're only talking about one man—"

"We're not talking about a man!" Montero cut him off. "We're talking about *Zorro.*" He moved to the window and peered outside in the direction of the burning Z. "And he *knows.*"

Love followed Montero to the window. While the two men had their backs turned to the desk, Alejandro silently drew his rapier and carefully lowered it until its very tip rested against the map. A small thrust and the point pierced the parchment, skewering it so that it could be lifted from the desk.

"Santa Anna is to arrive in two days," Montero was saying, "and Zorro is here tonight. There's more than coincidence at work, Captain Love. I erred by not having him killed long ago."

"He won't stop us," Love replied confidently. "You have my word."

Montero whirled on him. "Of what use is your word to me? I brought you here to safeguard my operations, and just now Zorro is jeopardizing my entire future! What have I experienced since returning to California but setbacks?" He pointed out the window. "Mark my words, Love, Diego de la Vega is out there somewhere, intent on destroying my plans. Or on killing me!"

"There's no proof that it's de la Vega," Love countered.

"No proof you say? What of the prisoner who escaped Talamantes? What of the guard stationed outside this very room who claims to have been knocked unconscious last night?" Montero's voice was shrill with indignation.

Love snorted a laugh. "I don't buy it. From the looks of things, he made off with about twenty glasses of wine, drank himself silly, and hit his head when he passed out." Distractedly, Montero clenched his interlocked hands in nervous anticipation. "What if Santa Anna is made aware of what I've been doing under his nose for the past twenty years?" His face grew pallid. "What if at this moment he is riding north with an occupying army rather than a document of purchase?"

Love shook his head. "You heard Don Luiz: Santa Anna's coming here for the gold."

"And suppose he should learn of the mine *after* the transaction? What's to prevent him from reneging on the transaction and mounting an invasion? I'm certainly not about to barricade myself inside the presidio like those fools at the Alamo."

Love mulled it over for a moment. "If that's all that's troubling you, why not just get rid of the evidence? The mine's played out, anyway. All we'd have to do is rig the necessary explosives and bury the whole works."

Montero scowled. "We can't possibly evacuate hundreds of workers by noon tomorrow."

"Then don't move them." Love paused. "Leave no witnesses."

Montero's eyes clouded over momentarily, then he spoke again in a calmer voice. "Your repeated failure to capture Zorro disappoints me, Captain. Or is it that you are a secret ally of Diego de la Vega—a traitor in my midst? If so, if you have betrayed me, I promise you a death beyond your wildest—"

"You're wrong to question my loyalty," Love said sharply. "I have as much at stake as you have. You lose a territory, I lose command of an army."

Montero seemed to retreat into himself. Consolidating the documents on the desk, he handed everything to Love. "Lock these away in your quarters. I must speak with Elena."

"And the mine?"

"Do whatever you think is required."

Love watched him leave the study, then he himself exited with determination.

Alejandro dropped quietly to the floor, folded the map, and tucked it into his belt. A glance out the window revealed that the grounds were now swarming with guards.

Love stormed down the hallway. After all he had done at the mine and elsewhere, to be accused of betrayal was almost more than he could endure. What, if not loyalty, had stopped him from helping himself to Montero's gold or spreading word of the find? Loyalty and faith in Montero's promise that he would one day serve as military commander of California—destined to be among the richest nations of the Americas.

Aimlessly sorting through the documents he had been handed, he cursed himself for having failed to anticipate just such a reaction from Montero regarding Zorro. Three years earlier, shortly after arriving in Los Angeles, Love had begun to hear rumors of how a flamboyant outlaw had undermined Montero's tenure as commandant, robbing him of what he robbed from the peons, fomenting dissent, and generally foiling Montero at every turn. Not until the end of his command had Montero discovered that his rival was actually a highly respected nobleman named Diego de la Vega. Unknown to any but a handful of devoted soldiers, he had had de la Vega imprisoned, but the ghost of the Fox had obviously been haunting him for the past twenty years. And now someone masquerading as Zorro was trying to subvert Montero by carving *Z's* on walls and burning them into the surrounding hillsides. Love refused to believe that it was de la Vega, escaped from Talamantes. But that hardly mattered. The outlaw had to be stopped—

Instinctively he came to a sudden halt and began to leaf through the documents with diligence. The map was missing. It was possible that Montero had taken it with him. But—

He whirled and hurried back to the study, calling out to any guards within earshot. Throwing open the door, he found himself face-to-face with a masked figure, who seemed to have manifested out of the very darkness. Before he could even register a reaction, the tip of the devil's rapier was pressed hard to his throat.

"Do as I say, or your mother will lose a son." Zorro forced him back against the hallway wall and relieved him of his sabre. "Move," the outlaw commanded, driving him backward down the hallway, Love's saber now at Zorro's hip and Zorro's blade still at Love's throat. Love locked gazes with the outlaw, trying to discern the features of the face beneath the mask.

Zorro rushed him into the intersecting hallway, then he abruptly ordered Love to stop. Love suspected that they had walked right into the line of fire of some of the guards that had answered his call.

Zorro dragged Love back around the corner, pressing his own back to the wall. "Your captain is not invulnerable to bullets," he shouted to the guards. "Lay down your weapons and approach." When the men hesitated, Zorro pricked the skin of Love's neck, snarling, "Tell them."

"Do as he says!" Love said through gritted teeth. He heard the sound of the flintlocks striking the floor, then approaching footsteps.

"Halt!" Zorro said when the pair had reached a set of tall windows that overlooked the inner courtyard. "Now, turn and face the windows." When the guards had obeyed, Zorro steered Love around the corner once more and bade him stop. "Bend over and touch your toes," he ordered the guards, with a note of jest in his voice. "I know it's difficult, what with your well-fed bellies, but do it anyway."

Again, the flesh of Love's neck paid a price for the guards' hesitation. "Do as he says!" Love repeated.

The soldiers bent at the waist, their ample rears extended into the hallway and their faces pressed to the panes of glass. Zorro manuevered Love into a position between the guards; then, without withdrawing his blade from Love's neck, Zorro kicked with his right leg, then his left, sending the guards head first through the windows. Glass shattered, wood splintered, and Love heard the agonized grunts of the two men as they struck the paving stones of the courtyard below. Zorro then pricked Love back into motion, in the direction in which the guards had first appeared. When they arrived at the flintlocks, Zorro ordered him to turn around and face forward.

Cutting his eyes to a brass-framed wall mirror, Love watched the Fox deftly sheath his sword and stoop to claim the guns. Behind Zorro, Love spied three more guards appear at the far end of the hallway, raising their flintlocks to their shoulders as they ran. Zorro caught sight of their reflection in the looking glass and, without turning around, laid the guns across his shoulders and triggered them simultaneously.

Two of the guards jerked backwards and fell, even while their weapons were discharging. Hardball rounds slammed into the hallway ceiling, shattering plaster and felling a chandelier, which crashed down on the head of the third man. But by then Love himself was in motion. Whirling on his heel, he slammed Zorro to the floor, then raced down the hallway toward the fallen men. He had thought to take up one of the flintlocks, but with Zorro already giving chase, he instead grabbed hold of the lead man's sabre and turned to meet his captor.

Their blades met angrily with a piercing ring. Zorro was fast with his rapier, but Love made use of the heavier sabre to drive him backwards down the hallway. Closing on him, body-to-body, Love backhanded Zorro across the face, sending him spinning into the wall. At the same moment, Montero—also armed with a sword—appeared from around the corner, his face pale with fright as he beheld the specter of his nightmares before him. But his appre-

171

hension lasted for only a moment. Recovering, he boldly flourished his blade and moved swiftly to join Love in the fight.

Caught between the two of them, Zorro drew Love's sabre from his belt and, with a weapon in each hand, parried the scything blades of Love and Montero as they fell in on him, time and again. But Zorro knew that he couldn't maintain the defense. Availing himself of the opportunity, he hurled himself backward through the doorway into a darkened room.

Love and Montero charged in after him, but, as he peered around, Love instantly grasped that they had lost the momentary advantage they had enjoyed. Only vague shapes were discernable in the scant candlelight filtering in from the hallway. Was that a chair in the corner of the room or a crouching man? A shadow fell across the windows in the far wall, but was the shadow cast from inside or outside? Love swung edgily to sounds and perceived movements on all sides. Then, all at once, a blade clanged against his sabre, nearly knocking it from his hand, and the fight was renewed.

Directly in front of Love, someone crashed into a settee and slipped to the floor. Before he could discern who it was, Love's own feet snagged on a carpet and he himself went down, his sabre extended in front of him. Sudden movement off to his left sent him pivoting just in time to parry a hammering downward slash. He threw himself to one side, scrambled to his feet, and counterattacked with a series of rapid strokes that sent his opponent backwards against the wall, then down to the floor.

"So, the legendary Fox has met his match," Love said triumphantly.

His sabre was probing for soft places in the body at his feet when three more guards hurried in. A torch in the hand of one them spilled flickering light across the room, revealing Montero at the end of Love's blade.

"You fool!" an ashen-faced Montero gasped. "He has escaped!"

Flirting With Danger

While the swords of Love and Montero clashed in the dark, Alejandro ducked into the adjoining room and quietly closed the door behind him. Recognizing where he was, he hurried to the balcony that overlooked the private courtyard, just in time to see Cadet Corporal Lopez and four other soldiers from the garrison rush into view below.

Alejandro turned to the sound of additional men filing in through the hallway. His only option was to chance an escape by way of the balcony. Keeping flat to the wall of the hacienda, he edged outside, seconds before the door to the room burst open. Throwing caution to the wind now, he raced for the far side of the balcony only to see a second group of soldiers hurrying up the courtyard stairs, swords at the ready. Spying Alejandro, the troops on both sides charged. Alejandro quickly calculated which group would reach him first.

"Excuse me, gentlemen," he said, "but I'm going to step out for some air."

He delayed until the last possible moment, then hurled himself over the balustrade into the courtyard. The soldiers collided in a tangle of arms, legs, and drawn blades.

Zorro's landing, although nimble, wasn't necessarily a silent one. Corporal Lopez and his contingent turned to the noise and attacked, immediately backing Alejandro against Montero's round table. Sidestepping the reckless assault, Alejandro slammed one soldier on the head with the pommel of his sword, then made use of the collapsed body as a ramp to the top of the table. There, he planted his hands on his hips and threw a laugh to the sky.

"A beautiful night to run someone through, eh, corporal?" He brandished his rapier at the suddenly nervous soldiers. "Which of you would like to be first?"

They came at him all at once, swarming from all sides, forcing him to dance as much as fight, as he leaped from hissing blades and diverted others with lightning-quick parries. Jumping straight up, he hooked one hand around the branch of the shade tree, so as to bring his feet into the fight.

He was still swinging one-handed from the branch, lashing out with his rapier and both legs, when Love and Montero rushed on to the scene to lend their support to the fray. With a powerful swing, Alejandro propelled himself over the heads of his assailants, landing close to Montero's outsize canvas map of the would-be Republic of California. As Montero and Love renewed their attack, he whirled and cut the cords that kept the map suspended, sending it billowing out and collapsing on top of them.

Keeping to the shadows of the eastern colonnade, Alejandro hurried for the perimeter wall, hoping that

Tornado would be waiting for him somewhere on the other side. He saw a ladder leaning against the edge of the tile roof and ran for it, with several soldiers in pursuit. The lead soldier made repeated stabs at him while Alejandro rapidly scaled the rungs. Hands clenched on the rails, Alejandro heaved, flipping the ladder over so that he was suddenly clinging to the underside.

Hanging from a rung, he repelled a second soldier with a kick, even as the first was contining to flail away at him. Then Alejandro flipped the ladder again, shaking the first soldier loose while managing to boot another one squarely in the face. Once on the roof, he scampered to the top of the wall and whistled for Tornado. But the horse either didn't hear him or didn't respond. Spurned, Alejandro made tracks for the stable, scurrying along the top of the wall like a tightrope walker.

Horses in their stalls whinnied and snorted in reaction to Alejandro's entrance. Slouching against a wall, he surveyed the mounts, wondering which would prove the swiftest. He had his eye on a piebald when the front door abruptly closed, muting the chaotic sounds of yelling and screaming outside. He drew his blade and steeled himself, waiting for his pursuer to show himself. Surprisingly, it was Elena who walked into view, dressed in a robe and wielding a rapier.

"Good evening, señorita," he said, showing himself and tipping his head. "We meet again."

She smiled, gamely it seemed. "Good evening, señor."

"Once more I warn you to take care. Dangerous men are about."

Her full lips tightened. "Men who impersonate friars, for example?"

"Ah, but who hasn't wanted to devote himself to the Church at some point in life?"

"The Church is no place for thieves, señor." She thrust out her hand. "I want whatever it is that you stole from my father."

Alejandro laughed, but he no sooner advanced a step when her sword came up, leveled at his heart. "Oh, come now, señorita, must we argue?"

"Not if you return my father's property."

His sidestep prompted her to attack with true intent—practiced and deadly. Taken off guard, he raised his weapon and leaped out of her reach. "I could tell you some things about your father, señorita, but I haven't the time. Nor have I the time to instruct you in the proper use of a sword."

She flourished the blade, making tiny circles in the air in front of him. "I hardly need your instructions, señor. I've had a blade in hand since I was four years old."

She moved in to engage, feinting adroitly, then succeeding in slashing his shirt. Again, he backed out of harm's way, fingering the gash. "I salute your skill, but I caution you about growing overconfident."

Again she attacked, answering his strokes with expert parries and swift ripostes. They dueled for several seconds before disengaging. Alejandro could tell that the robe was slowing her down, but he was astonished to see her shrug out of it. Shortly, she stood before him in a long, wide-strapped nightgown.

"You leave yourself uncovered in more ways than one, señorita." He advanced with a leap off his leading foot, feinting an attack only to pass by her and twirl, his blade slicing the nightgown to expose the smooth curve of her left hip.

"Well-made," she said

He eyed her bared flesh. "Indeed."

Undaunted, she took the fight to him, only to be driven back by countertimed glissades and remises. One strap of the nightgown cut, it fell away from her shoulder, revealing the upper swell of her breast.

"You're failing to catch the strong of the blade," he told her. "Soon you'll be leaving yourself completely exposed; then ripe for enfoldment." Leaning in, Alejandro quickly stole a kiss from her.

Elena grew incensed and renewed the duel, scooping up her robe and employing it as a cape to parry his thrusts, even snapping it into his face as a diversion. A series of quick slashes and one sleeve of his shirt dropped away.

"Quite impressive," he told her.

Her eyes fell on his shoulder and chest. "Indeed." Once again, Alejandro stole a kiss, flustering Elena.

Closing, she backed him against a bale of hay. When he tried to execute a body-to-body, she caught hold of his rapier with the robe, twisted it from his grasp, and sent it sailing across the stable.

"This may complicate matters," Alejandro said, as stunned as she was by the reversal.

Elena grinned and advanced. Trapped, he performed a backward somersault over the bale, losing his hat but managing to parry her attack by using his bootheels and the rowels of his spurs. Sparks flew, until at last he succeeded in trapping the blade between his crossed spurs. Rolling, he wrenched it from her hand, but she was quick to take up his sword and renew the offensive.

178

Breathing hard, he balanced her sword on his fingertips. "Lighter. It all but floats on the hand."

She paused to wipe sweat from her brow, her chest heaving. She moved to restore some dignity to the fit of her nightgown. "I'm sure you'll credit your defeat to the blade," she added cloyingly.

Elena lunged quickly, though awkwardly. He enveloped his own blade with her sword and snapped it to one side, where it stuck into the wall, bobbing up and down as if waving at them. Then, grinning slyly, he executed a flurry of precise strokes that further diminished what scant cover the nightgown provided, and, in the end, her dressing gown dropped to the floor.

"You fought bravely, señorita, but you are clearly undone."

Her nakedness notwithstanding, she held his gaze, defiantly, somewhat invitingly. He kept her on point as she pulled the gown up over her; then he began to back her toward the bales of hay. Drawing near so that he could feel his hot breath on her neck, Alejandro pressed her against the hay. When she could no longer move, she leaned back over a bale, her face illuminated by a shaft of moonlight entering through a window high up in the wall, her fiery eyes glittering.

"Do you surrender?" he asked.

"I warn you, señor, I'm still armed with a scream." Her voice was husky, throaty with both fear and excitement.

"I sometimes have that effect on women." He leaned to kiss her and met little resistance. Her moist lips parted, and as they separated, she stared deeply into his dark eyes. He leaned in once more, and as she raised her lips for another kiss, he suddenly angled to one side and retrieved his wide-brimmed hat from the floor, putting it on as he backed away.

"Good evening, señorita," he said, touching the edge of her blade to the brim of his hat. After yanking his own sword from the timber, he tossed her sword into the same post; then, leaping to a ladder and scampering up onto the loft, he was gone.

Elena asked herself whether her disappointment owed more to having been defeated or abandoned. She was still catching her breath and arranging the robe around her when the stable door opened and her father rushed in, followed by Captain Love, Corporal Lopez, and several other soldiers.

Astonished at her disarray, Montero moved in protectively to shield her from view. "What are you doing here?" he asked in alarm. "What happened to you?"

"Zorro," she said, swallowing hard. "I followed him here from the courtyard. "I fought him, but he got the better of me."

Her father's eyes widened further in shock. "You mean—"

"With his sword. Then he left."

Montero stood still for moment, oblivious to the frustration that punctuated her remark. "Did you recognize him?" he asked. "Was he a man of my age?"

Elena tugged her rapier from the post and slashed angrily at the air. "No, Father. He was young and . . . vigorous. Very vigorous."

Montero showed her a puzzled look, then turned to the sound of approaching horses. The squad of soldiers who had been sent to investigate the flaming hillside had returned.

"No sign of anyone," Elena heard the sergeant tell Harrison Love.

"We had an intruder," Love replied. "Take your

men and ride to the bridge to cut off his escape." He swung to Lopez. "Search the woods. Shoot on sight— even if you're not certain it's Zorro."

Elena felt a chill pass through her at hearing Love's ruthless order. She stared at her father's back, wondering just what "things" Zorro might have told her about him.

Tornado still hadn't answered Zorro's call by the time Lopez's squad exited the hacienda grounds at a full gallop, heading for the wooded ravine that bordered the hacienda to the east. The soldiers spread out at the tree line and began to weave through the willows, cottonwoods, and oaks, then formed up in a line, determined to undertake a more methodical search.

"Stay together," Lopez ordered. "Leave no openings."

Alejandro had made it no further than the underbrush on the near slope of the ravine. He waited until the mounted soldiers had disappeared into the trees before crawling back into the open and whistling for Tornado. This time, the horse surprised him by responding, emerging from the ravine at a quick trot and stopping within meters of him.

But Lopez had obviously heard the whistle as well, and was ordering his men to rein up and climb out of the ravine. Alejandro ran for Tornado as the distant hoofbeats grew louder.

"Time to prove that you're something other than handsome," he told the Andalusian. "Let's be off."

And Tornado was—without Alejandro, who made a desperate grab for the saddle only to be dragged a few meters and deposited in the underbrush once more. In hot pursuit of the riderless horse, Lopez's squad galloped past, but Alejandro was not to be outdone. Running the length of a lightning-struck tree whose bole still rested on a pillar of stump, he threw himself at the last horse in line, landing on its rump, behind the saddle. When the soldier twisted around, Alejandro sent him sailing from the horse and took his place at the reins.

Spurring the horse on, he came up on the next soldier in line and proceeded to unseat him in like manner; unseating riders with fantastic leaps and somersaults, he worked his way up the line of horses, until only Cadet Corporal Lopez was in front of him, unaware of what had gone on behind his back.

When one of the riderless mounts began to match strides with his own, Alejandro leaned over and grabbed hold of its reins; standing up on the saddle, he swung one foot onto the saddle of the second horse. He overtook Lopez in this fashion, passing over top of him, and thus obscuring the corporal's view of a low-hanging branch directly in their path. Alejandro let go of the reins of both horses, vaulted the branch, and landed balanced, on the saddle of both horses, while the hapless Lopez took the branch at full force and was toppled backward from his mount.

Alejandro caught up with Tornado just short of the bridge that spanned the river, and again changed mounts. Tornado ran like the wind for the bridge, but came to a snorting, rearing stop midway across. At the far side of the span waited half-a-dozen mounted soldiers. Hooves gamboling on the planks, Tornado spun through a full circle and had started to race back the way they had come when four soldiers rode into view, making fast for the bridge.

Alejandro drew his sword as Tornado wheeled

again in indecision. "Seven to one side, four to the other," he said. "Which will it be?" Tornado neighed and lunged toward the larger group. "Ah, so you want it to be a fair fight."

The remark alone seemed to bring the stallion to an abrupt stop. Ears back, eyes wild, Tornado turned and headed for the quartet.

"Make up your mind!" Alejandro yelled.

Tornado fell back to a skittish canter, then pranced to the railing and leaped over the side into the churning river below.

At the Montero hacienda an hour later, the former commandant listened in arrant disbelief to the soldiers' report.

"He did what?" Montero asked at last of the sergeant in command.

"It's true, *patrón*. He and the black steed jumped from the bridge. We stood watch for a long while without seeing either of them come to the surface."

"He is truly the devil's own son," Lopez said from within a headful of bloodstained dressings.

Montero looked sharply at Love. "And the map?"

The Texan shook his head.

"Captain, you recall what we spoke of earlier this evening regarding the mining operations?"

"I remember."

"Then I wish you to go about concealing the evidence as quickly as possible."

Love nodded. "I'll see to it."

Blinded by Revenge

ALEJANDRO PEELED OFF HIS WET CLOTHES WHILE Diego studied the sodden map of the mine. *"Caballo loco,"* he berated Tornado, who was calmly munching oats in his stall near the mouth of the cave. "Don't you *ever* do that again! You could have gotten us both killed. And worst of all," Alejandro plucked his one-sleeved shirt from his chest, "Zorro does not enjoy getting wet!"

"Forget about your outfit," Diego said, spreading the map out for Alejandro's inspection. "Tell me again about the mine."

Alejandro knuckled water from his eye and jabbed a finger at one of the map's abundance of cryptic symbols. "This is where they have found the mother lode. Northeast of the pueblo—about halfway to San Felicia Canyon."

Diego nodded. "I know that country."

"There are less than twenty guards. Nothing Zorro couldn't overcome." He grinned at Diego. "Or two Zorros, for that matter."

Diego didn't reply in kind. Folding the map, he moved away.

"The captives have been weakened by lack of food and constant work in the hot sun," Alejandro went on, "but they will surely join in the fight once they've been set free."

Diego looked at him. "I won't be going to the mine."

Alejandro's brow wrinkled. "What are you saying? Of course, you'll be going."

"There is something else I need to attend to," Diego told him. "Something I have waited twenty years to set right."

"You're making no sense. What about all the people Montero has enslaved and plans to bury?"

Diego's look softened somewhat. "They have you now."

Alejandro gaped at him. "Me? I can't battle twenty men by myself. Besides, you are the true Zorro. You were their protector. They believed in you. You can't turn your back on them now. Your personal business can wait."

"Don't tell me what I can and cannot do!" Diego shouted. "I gave my life to those people!" His anger turned to pain. "You think that being Zorro was all adventure and derring-do, but I lost everything, Alejandro. My wife, murdered before my very eyes. My child, stolen and brought up by my most hated enemy . . ."

Alejandro's eyes widened in sudden revelation. "Your daughter? Are you telling me that Elena—"

Diego cut him off with a nod.

Alejandro weaved in disbelief, extending his arms to the table to support himself. "I didn't understand. I should have, but . . ." He shook his head and looked at Diego. "So now you will exact your revenge on Rafael Montero."

"I will reclaim what is mine," Diego said.

Alejandro snorted. "Do you remember what you told me not two days ago—that we cannot change the past; that we cannot return the dead to life by acts of vengeance. Was that all so much talk?"

"You're too young to understand."

"To understand what—betrayal? All the work, all the training, all the wise words—for what? To learn to smile in the face of my brother's killer, while you make your own plans? You told me that I must wait for Harrison Love to enter my circle before I engage him. Isn't the same true with you and Montero? Isn't there more at stake here than revenge?"

Diego slapped the map against the palm of his hand. "This gives me the leverage I need against Montero. To safeguard his precious dream of an independent California, he will do whatever I ask rather than risk having this map fall into the hands of Santa Anna. He will tell Elena the truth about her past."

"And what then?" Alejandro asked. "You allow Montero to go through with his plan, in full knowledge of what he will do to those slaves when the purchase has been made?"

"I've taught you what you need to know to prevent that!"

"You've forged me to be your weapon, is that it? The sword you are too feeble to wield in your own hand?"

Diego stood to his full height. "I must look to my own heart. My daughter is my life, and I will do whatever it takes to protect her from the bloodbath that will follow Santa Anna's unveiling of Montero's treachery."

Alejandro stood his ground insolently. "I love your daughter as well. But I cannot put even her life above the lives of so many." He drew his sword. "Convince me that the fight has gone out of you."

Diego hesitated, looking towards the many swords resting in the rack. But he made no move toward them, only turning to face Alejandro in silence.

Alejandro sneered at him. "Perhaps one day you were a fine swordsman." He gave Diego one last, bitter look; then turned and strode defiantly out of the cave.

Montero and Love had spent the day finalizing the plan to make good on the delivery of the gold. A messenger dispatched by Don Luiz had arrived to say that Santa Anna wouldn't tolerate any delays. That night, in the private courtyard, Montero gazed at the patched and rehung canvas map of the territory. Love, descending the stairs from the balcony, found him like that, as if in the grip of a vision.

"We've got every inch of the countryside covered," the Texan reported, "from San Pedro to San Felicia Canyon, and from San Gabriel clear to Santa Barbara. If he shows himself . . ." Realizing that Montero wasn't listening, Love let his words trail off. "Are you all right?" he inquired.

"The map is still missing," Montero said, stating the obvious with an eerie calm.

"We'll get it back."

Montero cut his eyes to him. "In my lifetime?" When Love didn't smile, he added, "What if Zorro should show it to Santa Anna? Is your budding army prepared to make a stand?"

"A last stand," Love muttered.

"Then why do you bother to inquire if I am all right?" Montero bellowed.

Love allowed a moment to pass. "We'll find him."

Montero glowered. "I'm beginning to think that my horse could run this army better than you."

"I said I'll find him," Love shot back. "That means I will."

They were moving toward the archways that lined the courtyard when a voice called out of the dark, "Perhaps I can save you the trouble."

A rapier extended from the darkness of the arcade, its tip pressing into the soft flesh under Montero's chin. Montero winced and halted in his tracks. Love instantly reached for his sidearm, but stopped short of drawing when he saw the blade impress itself deeper into Montero's neck.

"Go ahead, reach for it, Captain," the voice taunted.

Love relaxed his arm.

"Who are you?" Montero asked carefully. "How did you get in here?"

"I'm on familiar terms with this house," said the male voice. "The balconies, the courtyards, your personal study . . ."

"Answer me! Who are you?"

The wielder of the rapier snorted a laugh. "The specter who has haunted you for half your life. The one who warned that you never would be rid of me."

The tip of the sword moved to Montero's collar, dragging it down until the fading zigzag scar was revealed.

"De la Vega," Montero gasped.

Love's eyes opened wide in surprise. "Zorro!"

Diego slowly emerged from the darkness. "We meet again, Rafael."

Montero stared at him in disbelief. "You . . . you are not the Zorro who was here last night," he managed.

"There are many who would gladly don the mask of the Fox, Rafael."

Montero straightened, audaciously. "You are too late, in any case. Even you cannot stop what has been set into motion."

"Ah, but I'm not here to stop you, Rafael. I've come for Elena. Send for her. I want her to hear the truth from your own lips, or Santa Anna will learn everything. Your choice is simple: the Republic of California or my daughter."

Montero's eyes brimmed with hatred. Love looked back and forth between the two men in utter bafflement.

"Call for her," Diego repeated, "or you will never call for anyone again." He sent the tip of the rapier deeper into Montero's flesh, almost piercing the skin.

Montero motioned to Love. "Find Elena. Bring her here."

Love worked his jaw. "Are you certain—"

"Bring her!"

Reluctantly, Love backed away, then disappeared into the arcade. Montero held Diego's gaze for a long moment. "If I die, the truth dies with me." His own words emboldened him. "Kill me and you rob Elena of the only father she has known for twenty years. For that alone, she would never forgive you."

Diego nodded. "I've already given that thought, and I'm prepared to take my chances." He withdrew the rapier ever so slightly. "You can't imagine the many ways I've dreamed of killing you, Rafael. I've imagined tortures that would sicken the Marquis de Sade."

"Is that so?" Montero said casually. "I've never given you a second thought."

Diego laughed ruefully. He was about to reply when Elena's voice rang out from the arcade. "Father!" She hurried into view, Love one step behind her, then stopped to glance first at the Montero, then at Diego.

"Bernardo! What are you doing here? Lower your sword at once."

Diego lifted his chin to Montero. "Tell her, Rafael."

Montero tightened his lips and stood his ground.

"Tell me what?" Elena asked stridently. "Please tell me what's happening!"

"Tell her," Diego barked, the rapier emphasizing the demand. "Tell her who her real father is."

Elena stared at Montero. "Father? What is he saying?"

Montero seemed on the verge of relenting when he quirked a thin smile. "Elena, this man is deranged. His own daughter died long ago, and now he seeks to claim you as his own. Why, just yesterday, he made the same claim of Don Hector's daughter—"

"Tell her how her mother died," Diego cut him off.

Montero looked at him. "Your daughter is gone, de la Vega. You must let go of the past."

"De la Vega?" Elena asked in astonishment.

Montero and Diego both turned to her.

"An Indian woman in the market told me—"

"Elena!" Montero shouted. "Leave us at once, do you hear me?"

Elena held firm, gazing at Diego. "The Indian woman said that Diego de la Vega was my father. I was told that my *niñera* used to hang something on my crib."

"Yes . . ." replied Diego, "your mother had her put fresh flowers there."

She frowned at him in confusion. "But you claimed to be . . ." She studied him through forming tears. "You're no more a servant than Alejandro is a caballero. Why did you deliberately deceive me?"

"Elena," Diego said again, lowering the rapier.

Vigilant, Love reached for his revolver. Catching

190

sight of it, however, Elena threw herself in front of Diego, just as Esperanza had on that fateful night long ago. Both Montero and Diego started toward Love, but it was Montero who reached him first, knocking the captain's arm aside so that the shot missed by a wide mark. Montero then backhanded Love across the face in a moment of uncontained wrath.

Diego held Elena, shielding her, as Love staggered backwards, more surprised than injured. Drawn by the shot, three guards rushed into the courtyard. Diego stepped out from Elena, his sword raised once again.

"Lower your blade," Montero hissed in warning, "or I will have no choice but to have you shot—even in the presence of my daughter."

Elena glanced at Diego. "Please, do as he asks."

Diego held her gaze for a moment, then nodded and dropped the sword. Two of the guards took hold of him, while the third snatched the weapon from the floor.

"Flowers," Diego said to Elena as the guards were leading him away. "Romania!"

Elena gave a confused start.

"She knows," Diego told Montero, just loud enough for him to hear.

"You're dead," Montero whispered back. He moved quickly to Elena, gathering her in his arms.

Glowering at Love, Elena pushed Montero away. "You would execute a man for nursing a delusion, Captain?" She then broke away from Montero, looking directly into his eyes, saying, "Or is there more truth to Don Diego's words than even you wish to admit, Father? I want the truth."

"You heard the truth, child. The man is insane. Now go to your room and we'll talk about all this in the morning."

She shook her head. "I'm not leaving until you tell me: Is Diego de la Vega my father?"

"I am your father, and will always be," Montero said harshly. "Now, go inside."

Elena whirled and hurried, sobbing, into the arcade.

Five meters down the corridor, Elena stopped to conceal herself behind an archway pillar. From the darkness, she wiped tears from her eyes and watched Captain Love and her father in the courtyard.

". . . ever, ever endanger my daughter again," her father was saying in a voice of controlled rage, "I will kill you—personally."

Love's reaction was one of defiance rather than regret. "And if I'd allowed him to tell her the plain truth about that night? Good God, man, why didn't you at least tell me who she was?"

Her father had no immediate answer. Moving toward the balcony stairs, he said, "Have the horses made ready. We'll leave for the mine immediately."

"It would be wiser to wait till dawn," Love said in a calming voice. "We still have plenty of time."

"You still fail to understand, Captain. Zorro is at large. And he will be there."

Elena waited for them to climb the stairway. A stillness descended over the courtyard, marred only by the incessant stridulation of cicadas and other creatures of the night. She lifted her face to the stars, asking herself what Diego de la Vega and now Captain Love had meant by *that night*. Instinctively, she understood that her own life had just taken a turn, and she grappled with what she would have to do now to bring herself back on course. Or if it were even possible to do so.

192

The Mask of Zorro

MONTERO AND LOVE ARRIVED AT THE CANYON just before dawn. The sun rose into a sparkling azure dome, bringing the scaffolding and platforms into sharp focus. Touched by the morning rays, a wagon loaded with gold bullion gleamed like a fire set in heaven. Montero and Love surveyed the area from the canyon rim and were pleased.

"If de la Vega's ally is here, he's disguised as someone other than Zorro," Love remarked while he was eyeing the workers and guards through a telescope.

Montero nodded, unconvincinced, then glanced at his pocket watch. "We have to be underway in an hour if we're to rendezvous with Santa Anna at noon. Until then, I see no reason for celebration."

Leaving Montero with the wagon, Love descended to the canyon floor to supervise the chain of prisoners who were transporting the last of the ingots from the storage room to the basket of a water-powered paddle wheel lift that had been erected at the summit of the scaffolding. Those guards who weren't hastening the transfer with whips and gunbutts were elsewhere in the canyon, unspooling fuses that ran from dynamite charges placed in each of the four tunnels. The fuses converged on a single fuse Love himself would light when the time was right.

In one of the tunnels, hampering the exodus of laborers and guards, an exhausted Indian lay unmoving, despite repeated blows from hands and whips. When the guard realized that he couldn't haul the man out himself, he called for the assistance of the friar, who was busy distributing water to those in need. His cowl raised, the friar went to the fallen man, ladling water from his bucket to the Indian's parched lips. The Indian stirred, then began to drink greedily. Looking up into the face of his benefactor, he glimpsed the mask of Zorro.

Zorro put his forefinger to his lips in a gesture of silence as he helped the man to his feet. Two of the Indian's workmates helped him the rest of the way.

Zorro soon found himself caught in the press of prisoners being hustled from the tunnel. Lagging behind the rest, he ducked behind an ore truck, where he pulled the cowl from his head and shrugged out of the robe. Pressed to the wall of the tunnel, he edged out onto the scaffolding. Below, several guards were herding scores of captives into the three cages that served as their quarters. Off to one side, the final load of ingots was being lifted by the paddle wheel to a platform at the canyon rim. On the platform stood Montero, who checked his pocket watch and waved a signal to Harrison Love.

Love returned the signal from the canyon floor, then spurred his horse toward the place where the four fuses were joined in a thick bundle. There, he dismounted and ignited the central fuse with a well-aimed shot from his Colt Patterson revolver.

Suddenly grasping that they were about to be buried alive by the ensuing explosions, the workers began to panic, screaming in terror and hurling themselves futilely against the bars of their cages as Love and the other guards mounted up and began to ride off. Seeing the lit fuse, Zorro calculated that he couldn't reach it in time to sever it, but he reasoned that he might be able to persuade Love himself to do so by threatening the arrival of Montero's precious bullion.

Stepping into the open, he raced boldly for the fuse, attracting the attention of two of Love's men, who raised their rifles and fired. With rounds ricocheting around him, Zorro leaped from a scaffold ladder to the safety of a nearby tunnel. Love, meanwhile, had reined up and was looking over his shoulder when Zorro showed himself again, running for a ladder that lead to the paddle wheel, while the two guards climbed toward him in hot pursuit.

Love galloped back to the burning fuse bundle and cut it cleanly with a single swing of his sabre. The prisoners fell back from the bars in collective relief as the Texan began to clamber up the scaffolding toward Montero and the bullion wagon.

"Secure the wagon!" Montero instructed guards on the platform, his voice echoing from the canyon walls. "Stay alert!"

Hardball rounds from half-a-dozen muskets buried themselves in the grit at Zorro's feet as he reached the top of the scaffolding and ran for the hub of the paddle wheel. Montero snatched a rifle from one of his men and added another report to the fusillade.

"He's on the wheel! Stop him!"

Before the guards could reach it, Zorro hauled up the ladder that led to the hub and jammed it into the outsize wheel. The water-driven hoop ground to a sudden halt, leaving the ingot-laden lift car swinging in midair, twenty meters below the rim. But Zorro knew that he had accomplished little more than a delay, and even now Montero and the guards were rushing the wheel, intent on freeing it up and promising to visit swift punishment on the one who had brought it to a halt. As two guards scampered onto the hub platform, Zorro swung down from one of the spokes, sending the pair plummeting into the canyon.

Their weapons reloaded, Montero and the guards opened fire as Zorro reappeared, suspended from his sword as he soared agilely down a tension cable anchored to the scaffolding, arriving just in time to confront the two guards who had finally completed their long climb from the canyon floor.

Montero stepped to the edge of the platform, pulled the butt of the rifle hard against his shoulder, and took aim.

"It ends here," he muttered.

At that moment, however, something struck the weapon from below, causing his shot to go high. A second blow from out of nowhere sent Montero to the ground. He rolled out from under the unexpected attack, then froze, almost in disbelief, as he recognized his assailant.

"De la Vega!"

Scrambling to his feet, Montero unsheathed his blade, ready to draw blood. But behind his old foe Montero noticed Elena, a pistol thrust into her waist sash.

"Yes, *I* released him from the cellar," she confirmed. "He could have escaped, but he said that he had unfinished business here."

Montero tightened his grip on the hilt of his sword and moved forward to engage Diego. "To the death, then," he snarled.

On the scaffolding, Zorro fended off the blades of the two guards who had pursued him to the top. Ridding one of his sword, he grabbed hold of the man and hurled him into the other; he then turned and began to scamper up a wooden chute that fed water from a holding tank to a system of sluices. Joined by a third, the two guards he had overpowered raced up after him. Zorro had enough of a lead on them to leap for the holding tank's pull chain while his adversaries were only halfway up the chute. A churning torrent of water gushed from the tank, instantly filling the chute and sweeping the guards down the way they had come and off the scaffolding entirely.

The momentum of Zorro's leap to the chain carried him past the holding tank to another section of scaffolding. But no sooner did his boots hit the planking than another guard advanced on him, this one wielding a double-bladed axe. Zorro crouched as the axe flew toward him, missing, only to thud deeply into one of the holding tank's support ports. The guard was still coming at a fast clip, however. Zorro sprang forward to meet the man, whose wild charge was easily turned against him. Zorro spun and flipped the guard over his back, sending him lurching into the same post that now held his weapon fast. Impaled on the axe, the guard stiffened in what seemed like outraged wonderment, then slumped, as if suddenly deflated.

Rapid footfalls on the planking brought Zorro about-face in time to see Love rushing toward him, his sabre raised for a strike.

"One question, Captain Love," Zorro said, mounting a defense. "Where would you like *your* head displayed?"

Love gritted his teeth and charged. Zorro parried his powerful strokes but found himself unable to mount an effective counterattack. Slammed back against a support post, he ducked just in time to avoid a deadly thrust of Love's sabre. Love swung again, and Zorro rolled, losing his hat but nimbly coming to his feet to engage Love as he followed up with a succession of slashing blows. For a moment, their swords locked and they stood eye to eye with one another. Zorro snapped his sword forward, knocking the Texan backward off the walkway.

Love twisted in a desperate attempt to regain his balance, but momentum was against him and he went over the side, tumbling down the slope and crashing into the side of the outbuilding that contained the ore smelter. Zorro tracked him for a moment, then turned his attention to the canyon floor, where Love's contingent of guards had returned and were hurrying for the scaffolding. When he glanced back at the smelter, Love was hidden somewhere behind the boiler's various flywheels and controls, so he threw himself onto the slope, taking giant steps down the loose grit and ultimately coming to a rest against the side of the building.

Musket fire from Love's men drove Zorro for the door, where he drew his dagger and edged inside. A blast of heat immediately struck him from the furnace and the vats of molten dross. From somewhere in the building came the squealing sound of a valve-wheel being turned, and all at once the steam furnace began to shudder on its mounts. Zorro hurled himself through the door and back out onto the scaffolding seconds short of an explosion that blew away the front of the building, along with four hapless guards positioned nearby.

Zorro made a daring leap for the water chute and tumbled down it through a cloud of flaming debris, as airborne pieces of the building set fire to various portions of the scaffolding. He landed hard on a ore-train ramp, narrowly missing the car itself. He came to his feet running, only to find his way blocked at both ends by guards.

Overhead, a large rock-filled crate dangled by a thick rope from a pulley. Zorro lunged for it as the guards charged, successfully severing the rope before either contingent reached him. The crate fell, slamming into the tracks with such force that the two guards at one end of the ramp were catapulted clear over Zorro's head into the ore car. Quickly, Zorro put his shoulder to the car and sent it hurtling down the ramp toward the guards at the far end, who were forced to leap from the scaffold to avoid being run over.

Looking up, Zorro saw Love dashing from what remained of the outbuilding onto the scaffolding one level above him. Billowing smoke from below revealed that the base of the scaffolding was in flames.

Paralyzed by quandary, Elena watched Montero and Diego duel. Her shaking hand tightened on the grip of her pistol, but, uncertain of her target, she could not bring herself to fire. The father she knew, in battle against a man who had emerged out of the past to claim her as his child . . . Was Diego a victim of his own imagining, as Montero maintained, or had Montero been deceiving her all these years? The words of the Indian woman returned to her, as did the vague memories the romania flowers had provoked. And there was the sound of Diego's voice, which had conjured flashes of a past she might have known. . . . But even those things didn't settle the question of her upbringing. Certainly Diego and Esperanza had been husband and wife, but that didn't mean that Montero couldn't have been her father. The infant de la Vega had not died in the fire that had ravaged the hacienda; but since Diego had also survived, how had she come to be raised by Montero, and where had Diego been for the past twenty years?

Their rapid ride to the mine had scarcely allowed for shouted exchanges, let alone conversation. On the two occasions they had stopped to water the horses, she had asked him for an explanation, only to be told that it was something she needed to hear from Montero's lips; that Montero could put all matters to rest. Instead, Diego had told her about Montero's deal with Santa Anna to purchase California with the blood of slaves.

That she could not bring herself to champion either the one or the other told her something of the depth of her instincts toward Diego, and just how much damage had been done to her bond with Montero. But, now, what with the deadly clashing of their swords, there was some chance she might never learn the truth.

As aged and frail as he sometimes looked, it was clear that Diego was the superior swordsman. His blade moved in ways that her eye could not begin to follow, and it amazed Elena that Montero was even able to defend himself. Finally, however, the surety of

Diego's footwork and the power of his strokes got the best of Montero, and he was disarmed.

Diego held him at sword's point, his arm tensed and trembling. "Now I am at last free to kill you," he said through his rage.

"No!" Elena screamed, the word escaping her as she rushed to Montero's side. "Please, no!"

Diego cut his eyes to her briefly but kept his rapier pressed to Montero's throat; then he eased the blade away.

Elena risked another step toward Montero, to beg him to reveal all that he knew. But before she realized what had happened, he had grabbed her around the neck, tugged the pistol from her belt, and was holding it to her head. In that moment she knew the truth.

"Drop your sword," Montero ordered Diego.

He did so without hesitation, his eyes on her rather than on Montero. In Diego's face, she saw the genuine love of a father for his daughter, rather than the overprotective hovering that had masqueraded as love from Montero.

The former commandant of Los Angeles snorted a laugh. "You're a fool, de la Vega. I would never have hurt her."

"And I would never have taken that chance," Diego replied.

Montero shoved her aside and leveled the pistol at Diego.

An urgent "No!" escaped Elena now, as she lunged, hoping to spoil Montero's aim. She was not entirely in time; hit in the side, Diego spun and fell to the ground.

Glaring monstrously at her, Montero twisted her around and sent her crashing into the platform's railing. Her head struck something and she saw stars;

but through the illusory scintillations she could discern Diego staggering to his feet, rapier in hand and blouse slick with blood. There was no confusion as to whom she prayed would prevail. . . .

Thick, choking smoke from the fire at the base of the scaffolding was enveloping the imprisoned laborers. High on the scaffold, Zorro had abandoned his pursuit of Love and was climbing down toward the nearest of the cages when the captain ambushed him from behind. They fought furiously for a minute, moving first one way, then the other, but ultimately taking the duel to the end of a truncated walkway, where the fire raged behind them and the arrested lift car dangled below.

Flicking his blade, Zorro slashed Love's cheek once, then again and again. With each cut, the Texan fell back on the jouncing planks, but he was beyond feeling pain. Love lunged and Zorro delivered a final slash that puzzled Love enough to stop him. Slapping a hand to his cheek, he brought it into view in front of his face.

"An M—" Zorro said, "—for Murieta."

Love grinned madly. "Nobleman, renegade, and bandit. Three identities, one death."

Zorro backhanded Love with the hilt of his sword and sent him sprawling. But Love retained hold of his sabre and swung it as Zorro moved in—not at the Fox, however, but at the rope that bound the unsupported end of the walkway. Unsecured, one plank sprang up, whipping into Zorro's face and knocking him backward toward the edge of the scaffolding. Zorro leaped at the last moment, managing a safe landing atop the stalled lift but losing his sword in the process. Seemingly without concern, Love followed him down, sabre in hand as he hit the roof of the swaying car, directly opposite Zorro.

"This time, by God, I'll have your head."

"I doubt very much that God listens to you," Zorro replied as Love pounced.

Both hands clamped on the platform railing, Elena dragged herself to her feet. Several meters away, Diego—her real father—and Montero were locked in combat. Below, Zorro and Love had faced off on the dangling elevator. And far below them, flames were racing toward the caged captives, whose screams for help could be heard even on the rim of the canyon.

"Elena!" Diego shouted to her in the midst of battle. "You must do what you can to free them!"

Torn, she finally gave her head a clearing shake and started down the scaffolding. Fiery heat and thick smoke besieged her as she descended. Engulfed in flames, a huge section of walkways, ore car tracks, ladders, and stairways collapsed and fell in a blazing heap to the canyon floor. Burning timbers crashed to the ground, one of them reigniting the bundled fuse Love's sabre had severed earlier on. Almost at once, the sputtering flame spread in four directions, heading fast for the tunnels.

Weakened by loss of blood, it was all Diego could do to hold on to his rapier while Montero repeatedly hacked away at him. Against a ferocious attack, Diego fell to one knee alongside the bullion wagon, then fully to the ground as Montero hammered away with his sword, as if to beat him into the earth once and for all. Diego's rapier was soon flung from his grasp.

Diego pressed himself to the wagon as Montero

moved in to deliver a killing stroke. Anticipating the swing, Diego ducked at the very last instant, and instead of Diego, Montero's blade found the wagon's harness straps. Spooked, the horses reared, then raced off while Diego hauled himself up into the wagon's bench seat.

Again, Montero raised his sword and advanced, certain that he had Diego at his mercy. Diego rolled, escaping the blade as it bit deeply into the wooden seat. Yanking the sword free, Montero swung and stabbed at his quarry, but time and again Diego managed to twist away from the blade. Forced to the far end of the bench, he made a desperate lunge for the wagon's handbrake and released it. Instantly, the heavily laden wagon rolled backward, out of Montero's reach.

For a moment, Montero gazed at the departing wagon in what might have been amused disbelief; then he stormed boldly after it—unaware that the severed harness had become entwined around his feet. Encountering a large stone, the bullion wagon bucked and Montero's legs were suddenly swept out from under him. He pawed the ground, then began to scream as the wagon gathered speed on the downslope, closing on the rim of the canyon. . . .

Atop the lift, Zorro evaded each maniacal slash of Love's sabre. Then, with an abrupt crouch and a swift pivoting sweep of his right foot, he dropped Love on his behind. The breath knocked from him, Love made a plosive sound and lost his grip on the sabre. The weapon landed flat on the lift, and rolled over the edge; but Zorro rolled as well, and, reaching out, succeeded in snatching it in midair.

Losing his focus to rage, Love growled and heaved

himself back onto his feet. Spying Zorro flat on his back with one arm outstretched over the edge of the car, he strode forward in a crazed, lumbering way, just as Zorro was extending the captured sabre in front of him. Impaling himself on his own blade, Love came to a dead stop, his hands gripped around the sabre where it pierced him, just below the heart. Love remained standing on quivering legs for a moment, clinging to the elevator's rope for support, grimacing in shock and pain. His hate-filled eyes held Zorro's masked, seemingly indifferent gaze. Then all the breath went out of him and he collpased to his knees.

Zorro barely had a moment to appreciate his victory. Reacting to a clamorous noise above him, he looked up to see the bullion wagon plunging over the rim of the canyon, loosing a storm of gold ingots as it fell. Behind it, tied by his legs, came Montero, shrieking like a banshee. Zorro let go of Love's sabre and pulled his whip from his belt. Snapping the whip around a nearby scaffolding beam, he swung out into the air a moment before the wagon struck the lift, sending it, Love, and Montero crashing to the canyon floor.

Armed with two single-shot pistols she had taken from dead guards, Elena finally completed her long descent of the burning scaffolding. Her face was smudged with dirt and grease and she was breathing hard from exertion and smoke. Far behind her something heavy smashed to the ground, but she knew she couldn't stop to worry about what it was. Already halfway to their respective tunnels, the four diligent fuse flames were closing rapidly on the dynamite charges. The prisoners were distraught.

Elena sprinted to the nearest cage and shot the lock

open. Men and women streamed through the door, nearly knocking her down in their mad race for cover. Breaking free of the surge, she ran to the second cage and there discharged the second pistol. Again, men and women streamed through the door in panic, momentarily catching her up in their flight. But again she managed to break free and dash for the final cage.

Quick glances to either side revealed that the four fuse flames had disappeared into the mouths of the tunnels.

With both pistols discharged, Elena searched frantically for a way to open the lock of the third cage. In mounting hopelessness, she began to bludgeon the lock with the wooden grip of one of the pistols, but to no avail. Then, out of nowhere, a hammer suddenly fell on the iron lock, shattering it. She looked up to find Zorro standing over her, smiling.

Staring up into his dark eyes, a moment of recognition washed over her fluttering heart, "Alejandro . . . ?" she asked.

"No time to lose," he said, reaching for her hand.

They joined the fleeing prisoners in a furious race for safety as the fuses reached their destinations and the entire canyon was enveloped in a deafening storm of rock and dust.

A New Destiny

WITH THE SCAFFOLDING DEMOLISHED AND BURIED under countless tons of debris, it was a long, hard climb to the canyon rim. The gold was also buried, embraced once more by the very ground from which it had been dug.

Even while the dust was still settling, Elena and Alejandro searched frantically for Diego, finding him at last close to where the bullion wagon had gone over the side. Elena kneeled down beside her mortally wounded father, lifted his head, and ladled a bit of water into his mouth. Diego drank, then moved the ladle aside to look at Alejandro.

"Is it finished?" he asked weakly.

Alejandro nodded grimly. "It is finished."

Diego smiled with difficulty. "But not for Zorro, Alejandro. Evil is not so easily dispatched from this world. Alta California will know others like Montero. It is both your curse and your destiny to thwart them when they appear."

Alejando gazed out across the canyon. In that open

country where one could easily see past and future—the course that had been traveled and the road that lay ahead—the momentous nature of the events of the recent weeks seemed to crowd in on him. Deprived of everyone he held close—Joaquin, Jack, and now Diego, the mentor he never asked for, the father he never had—Alejandro was uncertain of his course. The past twenty years suddenly seemed like a dream. It was as if the spirit of the past had reached across time to amend injustices and to resolve matters that had never been laid to rest. For one moment, past and present had been brought together to create a future that otherwise might not have been. Alejandro understood that he had been forged into a righteous instrument; and that he had acted nobly and selflessly, as Don Diego had taught him. In that, his life had gained meaning and a purpose it had previously lacked.

"Then, so be it," he said at last.

Diego's eyes moved to Elena. "My beautiful daughter, fate plays strange tricks on us. Just when I find you, I lose you again."

She shook her head, wetting his face with her tears. "You'll never lose me—Father."

Diego stroked her cheek with his fingertips. "All I've ever wanted was to hear you say that word."

Elena took his hand between hers and brought it to her lips.

Diego's wan smile broadened. "You were right about your mother, *querida*. You so resemble her . . . her eyes, her smile, her spirit. And I know there's one thing she would have wanted for you." He placed Elena's hand atop Alejandro's.

Having lost not one but two fathers, Elena felt that the underpinnings of her life had been swept away, and though she could take some consolation in the fact that the truth of who she was had been revealed to her, she felt bereft, orphaned, unsure of just what steps to take on the long road ahead. She glanced cautiously at Alejandro, wondering if he was someone with whom she could make that start toward a new beginning.

Diego coughed harshly. "People will always need a hero to rally behind, Alejandro. Wear the mask proudly and, when the time comes, bestow it upon one you deem worthy—as I have." His voice trailed off. His breath rattled in his chest and he died in the arms of his daughter, who wept over his body for all that her life might have been. . . .

His own face masked with grief, Alejandro held Elena and cried silently with her. In the solace of each other's arms their apprehensions diminished, and in that moment the future seemed assured.

The prisoners began to set out for Los Angeles, trading smiles as they moved past Alejandro and Elena into the vast high desert landscape. The sky was dazzlingly clear, and it seemed that one could see forever.

Epilogue

*L*IGHTNING SPLIT THE SKY, THUNDER SHOOK THE earth, and then all was quiet," Alejandro pronounced in his most dramatic voice. "The great paladin known as El Zorro was gone. The people of the kingdom gave him a hero's funeral, the most elaborate anyone had ever witnessed."

Alejandro glanced at the crib to see if his son was still paying attention. The infant stirred under its wrappings and waved one tiny hand in the air, as if in distress.

"Ah, do not worry, little Joaquin," Alejandro said, relaxing his sword and going down on one knee alongside the crib. "Wherever great deeds are remembered, your grandfather lives on. For there must always be a Zorro. And someday, when he is needed, we will see him again."

Peace had reigned in Los Angeles during the time since the death of Diego de la Vega. Robbed by the land itself of the gold he had expected to receive from Rafael Montero, and with mounting problems of his own at home in Mexico, President Santa Anna lost all interest in the future of Alta California; and as word had spread of Zorro's heroic deeds at the mine, Peralta and the other dons, realizing the selfishness of their deeds, relinquished their short-lived dreams of an independent California and returned to their lives as complacent cattle ranchers and *hacendados*.

Having inherited Montero's Los Angeles holdings as well as those of the de la Vega family, Elena had eventually become one of the wealthiest landowners in that part of the territory, and after a courtship judged brief by nearly everyone's standards, she and Alejandro had married. Joaquin was born a year later.

Alejandro's fine clothes and silver-pommeled saddle were seen by many as evidence of Elena's success in turning the former horse thief into a true *caballero,* but Elena herself would have been the first to admit that fresh wrappings were scarcely enough to contain her husband's brash spirit.

Grinning down at his son, Alejandro raised himself to his full height. "On his fearsome steed Tornado, Zorro would scour the countryside for evildoers," he continued in bold voice, pantomiming a mad gallop through the desert scrub. "Riding like the wind itself, his enchanted sword blazing in the sun!" He flourished the blade and made a skillful leap onto a nearby chair. "Leaping, jumping, swinging through the air!" He launched himself from the chair, caught hold of the window drapes, and alighted on his feet halfway across the room, brandishing the rapier against a host of invisible opponents.

"Fighting like a lion! Fighting like a tiger!" Executing a tight spin and a perfect thrust in the direction of the doorway, Alejandro found Elena watching him, the skeptical look in her eyes parrying him expertly.

"Fighting . . . as safely as possible," he finished in a more subdued tone, the sword angled harmlessly toward the floor.

She glanced at Joaquin and arched an eyebrow. "This is your idea of putting the baby to sleep?"

With purposeful sheepishness, Alejandro returned to the crib. Leaning over, he kissed the child on the forehead. "Sweet dreams, my son." Then he straightened and went to Elena, caressing her cheek with the back of his fingertips. "And you as well, my beautiful wife."

Elena pulled away from his tender kiss to show him a playful smile. "And when I dream, what face shall I give to this dashing rogue, El Zorro?"

Alejandro grew serious. "He has been different men, it is true, but he has loved you as each of them."

Elena exhaled deeply. "And the one who now wears the mask . . . do you know where I might find him?"

Alejandro grinned. "You know how Zorro is, *querida*. He could be anywhere."